MY FUNNY FRANKENSTEIN

A PARANORMAL MYSTERY ADVENTURE

MONSTERS OF JELLYFISH BEACH 4

WARD PARKER

MAD MANGROVE MEDIA, LLC

This book is a work of creative fiction. Names, characters, places, and incidents either are products of the author's imagination or are used fictitiously. Any resemblance to actual events or locales or persons, living or dead, is entirely coincidental.

ISBN: 978-1-957158-19-8

CONTENTS

CHAPTER 1

1-800-MR-BOKOR

The chimes tinkled above the door of the Jellyfish Beach Mystical Mart and Botanica. A burly man with ebony skin, a shaved head, and a perpetual scowl walked in. It was Mr. Bokor, the voodoo sorcerer.

"Mandrake," he said in his deep, rumbling voice. "I need mandrake root."

"It's nice to see another member of the supernatural community visit our humble establishment," I replied, with only slight sarcasm.

"I ordinarily would never shop at a commercial establishment for my ingredients, but tonight I have no choice."

Madame Tibodet, who had introduced me to Mr. Bokor, was meeting in the back room with Luisa at the moment. Madame Tibodet was not fond of the sorcerer because he had turned her brother, Carl, into a zombie shortly after his death, and then demanded a large payment to return him to her instead of selling him as a servant to the highest bidder.

"I wasn't aware that mandrake was used in voodoo sorcery," I said.

"It isn't. Not in traditional sorcery. I have, well, my own custom experiments involving a bit of alchemy. Do you interrogate all your customers like this?"

"No. Sorry."

I went to the refrigerated cabinet in the rear of the store where we keep our rarer plants, herbs, and other fresh ingredients. Many spells require fresh mandrake root, rather than powdered.

"Is an ounce enough?" I asked.

"I'll ultimately need at least a pound, but I'll take what I can get tonight."

We had only three one-ounce bags. His gruff attitude convinced me to give him only two bags and save the third for a more pleasant customer.

"I can sell you two ounces now. We'll get more from our supplier next week."

He grunted and followed me to the front counter where we have our old-fashioned cash register next to a state-of-the-art electronic credit-card processor.

Suddenly, Mr. Bokor let out a high-pitched squeal that seemed incongruous coming from the large man.

"A land crab is attacking me! Why is a crab in here?"

"Please don't step on her!" I begged. "She doesn't mean you harm. She's a were-crab who is perpetually cranky while she waits to shift back into human form. The shifting is more of a molting process and quite unpleasant for her. And for all of us."

"Get it off me."

I reached down and pried the blue crab's claws off his ankle. She scurried beneath the counter.

I reminded Mr. Bokor what the total purchase price was. After he tapped his credit card, I tried to make small talk.

"Now that you're a customer, can I call you by your first name?" I asked.

"No."

"You're always on brand?"

He frowned.

"Bokor" is the term for a voodoo sorcerer. This gentleman, whose actual name I didn't know, incorporated under the name "1-800-MR-BOKOR." That name was on his credit card, and he used it for everything else.

His head jerked to the left as the sound of shuffling feet came from the hall leading to the back room.

Carl appeared. The deceased middle-aged Haitian professor had been reanimated by the very same individual standing across the counter from me.

Mr. Bokor's frown turned into a grimace. Perhaps, it was Carl's eau-de-coffin scent.

"Aren't you happy to see your creation?" I asked.

"Just because he's a zombie doesn't mean I created him. I'm not the only bokor around here."

"Madame Tibodet said it was you."

Carl moaned as he shuffled and lurched toward us. He didn't appear to recognize Mr. Bokor, but zombies have little in the way of facial expressions, so it was hard to read his feelings.

He walked past his maker without acknowledging him and picked up a ceramic cat from a shelf. Carl was obviously bored from sitting in the back-room meeting and needed a diversion.

Holding the ceramic cat like a real one, he moved to the corner where he petted the cat, making cooing sounds.

The moment would have been cute had Carl not been a zombie.

"He doesn't seem to recognize you," I said to Mr. Bokor.

"Why would he recognize me?"

"Because you turned him into a zombie."

Mr. Bokor shook his head. "He would be dead until the end of the ritual, then I would have confined him in a box. Are you certain that it was I who created him?"

"Madame Tibodet insists you did."

"I have created so many zombies over the years, I can't recognize them all. Especially when their faces are falling off."

"Carl! Where are you?" boomed Madame Tibodet's Caribbean-accented voice. "We are leaving now."

The woman, rather diminutive compared to her voice, stormed down the hall from the back room. She looked up in surprise when she saw Mr. Bokor.

"What are you doing here?" she asked, tilting her head, wrapped in a colorful scarf, sideways with suspicion.

"I have every right to come here to purchase supplies for practicing my faith."

"We'll see about that," she said, gently leading her zombie by the arm out the front door.

Mr. Bokor waited until she had pulled out of the parking lot before he, too, took his leave.

"Notify me when you get more mandrake root."

"I will," I said.

Luisa emerged from the back room. The beautiful Afro-Cuban's forty-ish face was taut with stress.

"Are you okay?" I asked.

"I can't believe it. Madame Tibodet wants to become a partner in the botanica."

"Really? She's just a part-time manbo," I said, using the term for a voodoo priestess.

"She thinks she can bring in tons of new customers based on word-of-mouth from her spiritual-counseling clients. She wants the store to cater more to voodoo practitioners. But I like it the way it is. When I first opened the place, it was centered on Santeria, but I expanded the offerings to voodoo, obeah, and various types of old-world witchcraft. I think we have the perfect balance now."

"I agree. And we don't need her to invest in the place. Not with all the backing we get from the Friends of Cryptids Society. In fact, I doubt they'd want us to have a partner who doesn't share their mission."

"They probably wouldn't. I just don't want to anger Madame Tibodet by turning her down outright. She provides a valuable service consulting with our voodoo customers and conducting the occasional service."

"You can always string her along until she loses interest," I suggested.

"Just what I'd expect you to say, since you hate confrontation."

"I was brought up by parents who never raised their voices."

I didn't mention that my birth mother relished confrontation. I'd had a few doozies with her since discovering she was alive, despite what I'd been told after I learned I was adopted.

"I guess we should find out what the Society thinks," Luisa said. "If they're against it, I can use them as an excuse."

It was my turn to close the shop, and Luisa soon went home to her daughters. I watched the clock for the next two hours after a brief flurry of customers came and went.

When I say I watched the clock, I also mean I listened to it. The tall, ancient grandfather clock in the corner was part of the botanica when Luisa first bought it from an obeah man. He said it was in the building when *he* bought it; the structure originally had been a pineapple packing house from the late 1800s. The clock had supposedly been built in the Caribbean from native mahogany wood.

The loud, severe ticking had taken me years to get used to. And just now, when it missed a beat, the blood drained from my face.

Had someone forgotten to wind the clock last night?

You see, there's a murky legend that this clock must never be allowed to stop or something tragic would happen. Exactly what, no one knew. It could mean the death of an individual or the end of the world.

Wanting neither, I rushed over to the clock and wound it by pulling on the counterweight chains housed in the slender vertical cabinet beneath the clock face.

Sure enough, it required quite a bit of winding. That meant no one had wound it last night. I could point the finger at Luisa because it had been her turn to close the shop.

At least the clock hadn't stopped. Well, it did miss a beat, but it was still running when I went to wind it. Nevertheless, I had a feeling of unease when I turned off all the lights, locked the doors, and closed the aluminum hurricane shutters we used to cover the display windows for extra security.

You're probably wondering why I didn't set the burglar alarm. Because we don't have one. I'm a witch, remember? Instead, I placed magical wards near the front and back doors. They would warn me of intruders. If the culprits were human, I'd call the police. If they were supernatural entities, well, then I would have to deal with them myself.

The parking lot at this end of the strip center wrapped around the rear of the botanica and was empty, especially since the fried-seafood takeout joint had moved away. Down at the other end, the ratty convenience store had a few cars out front. Here, there was only mine.

Wait, why was a car parked in the shadows by the dumpster?

And why was it giving me a feeling of foreboding?

Sure, I could have gotten into my car and left, but our contract with the Friends of Cryptids included the purchase of this property from our previous landlord. I was a part owner of this parking lot.

I felt obligated to check on the car. Hopefully, it was abandoned. Or perhaps it belonged to a customer of the convenience store.

Those hopes were dashed as soon as I got close enough to read the logo emblazoned across the side of the car.

1-800-MR-BOKOR

My heart missed a beat.

I cast a protection spell around myself and carefully approached the passenger side of the car. Rather than shine a flashlight into the windows, I used my telekinesis to flip the switch of the dome light above the front seat.

No one was inside. And the driver's-side window was open.

That the car was unoccupied calmed my fears. Maybe Mr. Bokor was in the convenience store buying scratch-off lottery tickets or binge-eating hotdogs.

But he had left the botanica over two hours ago.

I reached for the door handle. The car was unlocked. This did not bode well.

Nor did the dark crimson stains on the driver's seat.

I called 911 and reported finding the unlocked car belonging to my customer, who I'd last seen two hours ago. And that there appeared to be blood on the seat.

That was all that was required of a responsible citizen. All I needed to do was wait until the police showed up.

But my sixth sense told me Mr. Bokor was still on the premises.

I popped open the trunk and found it empty except for a mesh bag filled with baseballs. I didn't realize Mr. Bokor played the sport. Crouching on the asphalt, I peeked beneath the car. No corpse under there.

If that was truly Mr. Bokor's blood on the seat, then he must have been abducted. Or maybe, despite being wounded, he had escaped his attacker and walked home or to the hospital.

Or he succumbed to his wounds and was lying beneath a cocoplum hedge in someone's front yard.

My sixth sense tapped me on the shoulder and nudged me toward the dumpster. The bin was covered by a thick plastic lid hinged on the back and divided in half to make it easy for an individual to open one side and hold it up while tossing a bag of trash inside with the other hand.

One side of the dumpster was open, the lid hanging from its hinges at the back of the receptacle.

I inched closer to the open side. Already, I could smell death along with the rotting trash.

There, upon a pile of plastic garbage bags, lay Mr. Bokor. A rat squeaked and ran away, half of a convenience-store hotdog in its mouth.

If I was going to play amateur sleuth, I had to go all the way. I shined the flashlight from my phone on the body. Mr. Bokor was lying on his stomach, his feet closest to me. The visible side of his face was bloodied, as was his shirt.

Being a nurse, I knew where to find the popliteal artery in his leg. I pressed my fingers against his trousers behind his knee.

There was no pulse. No surprise, he was dead.

I called 911 again and told the operator I'd found a body. That would guarantee the police would get here faster. They should have shown up already, but I guess my first report hadn't sounded urgent enough.

"Why were you looking in the dumpster for the body?" the woman operator asked me.

"My sixth sense told me to look there."

"I would think your common sense would have told you to let the officers do that."

"What makes you think I have any common sense?"

CHAPTER 2
DOWN IN THE DUMPSTER

In Jellyfish Beach's minuscule detective bureau, Cindy Shortle drew the short straw and was assigned Mr. Bokor's murder case. When she arrived that night at the scene, she had warm words of greeting for me.

"You, again."

"Yes," I replied. "I go hand in hand with weird stuff."

"Fortunately, this crime doesn't sound like it involved Satanists defiling houses of worship."

"Hopefully not. But the victim was a voodoo sorcerer."

"Are you serious?" Detective Shortle was not happy.

"He's in the dumpster." I explained how I had discovered him.

Shortle had arrived at the same time as a uniformed officer, and they both looked at the body and the inside of the car.

"Looks like he was stabbed," Shortle said. "And his throat was cut."

"The perp must've been really strong to have tossed the

body in there," said the officer, who looked like he was well past retirement age.

"He could have climbed into the dumpster to escape his attacker."

"Nah," said the cop. "This dumpster has a tall lip. It would have been hard to climb in here, especially if he was bleeding out."

"His throat could have been cut when he was in here."

"Yeah, but he left a lot of blood in the car. He'd be too weak to climb into the dumpster."

"If you say so," Shortle said sarcastically. She'd had enough of this guy who believed his age and gender made him wiser than the young detective. It wasn't his place to come up with theories, anyway.

Shortle tried to ditch him by pulling me aside for questioning.

"You knew the victim?" she asked me. "Was he a customer of yours?"

I nodded. "He goes by the name of Mr. Bokor, but I don't know what his real name is. Bokor is what a voodoo sorcerer is called."

"Why was he here tonight?"

"To buy some mandrake root. He's never shopped here before, but I guess he couldn't find the mandrake elsewhere."

"But you said you knew him?"

"I met him once before in an unrelated matter."

I couldn't explain to Shortle that I had been investigating vampires at the time.

"Did he have an altercation with anyone tonight?"

"Not at the botanica."

"Do you know of anyone who had a grudge against him?"

I immediately thought of Madame Tibodet's resentment for what he did to Carl. But I didn't want to drag the woman and her zombie brother into this, much less explain it to Shortle. I doubted they were capable of murder anyway.

"I don't know of anyone who had a grudge against him," I said. "But I had the feeling his relations with clients might be contentious."

"What kinds of things would a voodoo sorcerer do for clients?"

"Things that could cause a lot of trouble."

Shortle shook her head in frustration.

"When are the crime-scene tech and medical examiner going to get here?" she asked the older cop.

"You've got to have patience in this job," he said, gazing into the dumpster. "You know, it's amazing how much waste our society produces. Look at all those perfectly good hotdogs the convenience store threw away."

The thought of the old hotdogs in the dumpster grossed me out more than the dead body on top of them. I asked the detective if I could go home now.

"Yeah, you can go. I know where to find you if I have more questions."

I ARRIVED home to three unhappy and hungry housemates—two felines and one reptile. The cats were trapped in the house, dependent upon me to open cans of cat food. The iguana, on the other hand, lived in my garage with a half-opened window. He was free to go outside and forage for plants and flowers and bugs.

"It's about freakin' time you got home," Tony, my witch's familiar iguana, said.

He could have foraged, but he preferred to give me a guilt trip. I retaliated by feeding the grateful cats first, before I poured a bowl of reptile chow for him from the pet store.

"You've got the stink of death about you," Tony said in his New York accent.

"You sure know how to flatter a girl."

"No, I'm serious. Is there anything I should know?"

"I found a murdered man, a customer, outside the botanica tonight."

"Wow. Santeria follower?"

"No. Voodoo. He was a sorcerer."

Tony expelled a hiss that I think was meant to be a whistle, but reptile mouths simply can't pull that off.

"I sensed a disruption in the supernatural frequency."

"Does that mean a supernatural creature killed him?" I asked.

"Not necessarily. He could have been in the middle of casting magic to protect himself, when—"

Tony's little foreleg made the gesture of a slit throat.

"How did you know his throat was cut?"

"I didn't. That was universal sign language for offing someone."

"Are you a suspect, Tony?" I joked. "Where were you this evening at around seven p.m.?"

"Eating your neighbor's flowers and pooping in their swimming pool."

"Forget that I asked. I'm fixing something to eat and going to bed."

Just as I was doing my own foraging for leftovers to heat, the doorbell rang. It was Mrs. Lupis and Mr. Lopez from the Friends of Cryptids Society of the Americas.

Great. There was no way they were here for a social call. And no, they weren't bringing me dinner.

"We've got a problem," Mrs. Lupis said.

"A big problem," said her partner.

"That bokor who was murdered was creating chimeras," Mrs. Lupis said. "Using magic and alchemy to bring to life creatures that are combinations of different species. Freakish things that shouldn't exist."

"Wait a moment, how did you know the bokor was murdered? The police are still investigating the murder scene."

"We have our sources and methods," Mr. Lopez said.

"You already knew about his chimeras," I said. "I sent you photos of a monkey-cat he had in his office. And a cat-dog owned by a vampire."

"Yes. Those are disturbing and violate too many rules to cite," Mr. Lopez said. "The cryptids we study were put on this earth by our creator. Mortal humans have no right to play God. But we've had other priorities and couldn't attend to this matter until now."

"We've learned things have gone way too far," Mrs. Lupis said.

"What do you mean?"

"We've seen evidence of human-animal chimeras."

"That is *so* wrong."

"Exactly," both partners replied in unison.

"Are you talking about a half-human, half-animal?"

"Not necessarily fifty-fifty," Mrs. Lupis said. "But we have no direct evidence, only hearsay."

"What kind of animal is it?"

"One account said it was an elephant," said Mr. Lopez. "Another claimed it was a French bulldog."

"The French bulldog is more believable," his partner said. "After all, Frenchies are so popular these days."

"Neither account is believable," I said. "In ancient mythology, maybe. But not in real life."

"You sent us a photo of a monkey-cat."

"I know. But a human? I have a hard time believing human features can be part of a chimera."

"When you mix black magic and alchemy, you'd be surprised what is possible," Mr. Lopez said.

"How many human chimeras are out there?"

"We don't know," Mr. Lopez replied. "More than one, we believe."

"I assume you stopped by because you want me to find them?"

They both nodded solemnly.

"The police will concentrate on finding the sorcerer's murderer," Mrs. Lupis said. "We need you to find where he was making the chimeras and if there are any still in captivity. Notify us when you find them. Before the police do."

"What if Mr. Bokor was killed by one of his chimeras?"

The partners exchanged a meaningful glance.

"We suspect that to be the case," Mr. Lopez said. "In particular, a human-animal chimera. Which creates even more urgency to find it before the police do."

I assured my handlers that I would do my best, and they finally left, allowing me to feed my face at last. Cold, leftover meatloaf never tasted so good.

But before I finished eating, my phone rang. I was going to ignore it, but the caller was Matt, so I answered.

"Hey, I heard chatter on my police scanner about a homicide," he said. "And the address was the same as your botanica's. You sound like you're okay, especially with your loud chewing. So, do you know anything about this homicide?"

"I'm the one who found the body."

"Oh, no! Are you really okay, then?"

"I guess." I recounted the gruesome details and what my visitors had told me.

"Chimeras? That's freaky. The cat-dog in Igor's mansion wasn't a one-off, then."

"No. I saw a monkey-cat back when Madame Tibodet and I visited Mr. Bokor's office. And if what I was told is true, there could be many more, including part-human ones."

"That's really disturbing. When I was a kid, illustrations of fauns and centaurs in books about mythology scared me."

"Well, I have to find out where these human-animal chimeras are. And you're going to help me."

"I am?"

"You're a journalist. You know how to find out stuff. I can go to Mr. Bokor's office and ask the other tenants in the shared suite about him, but they won't know anything valuable. Heck, I don't even know his real name or how to find it out."

"We can search the Florida Division of Corporations for his

company, and it should tell us his info if the company is registered under his own name."

"See, you know how to do this stuff."

To be honest, I'm adept at witchcraft, capable of solving mysteries, skilled at nursing, and pretty good at cooking. But when I'm using the internet, I'm anything but magical.

Matt called me again before I went to bed.

"I spoke to Shortle and another of my sources at the department about the murder," he said. "By the amount of blood in the car, it seems obvious that he was attacked while sitting in it. His attacker could have been in the passenger seat or was outside the car and reached into the open window to stab him and cut his throat. The window was open when you found him."

"What about the back seat?" I asked. "They could have been hiding back there and attacked him right after he got into the car."

"Yes, that's possible. He had defensive wounds in multiple places on both hands, consistent with being attacked from his right, his left, or from behind. Many of the wounds were puncture wounds—like from an ice pick."

"Why was an ice pick used instead of a gun?"

"Ice picks and knives don't leave a signature, like the rifling on a bullet, and there aren't any shell casings that the killer might miss and leave at the crime scene," Matt said. "Also, a weapon for stabbing is quieter."

"Not if Mr. Bokor screamed."

"No one claimed to have heard him."

"Do they know if he climbed into the dumpster to escape

his killer, or if he was tossed in there? Could he have climbed in there after losing so much blood?"

"That hasn't been determined, but the police aren't ruling it out."

"It would take a great deal of strength to throw him in there," I said. "Not many people could do it. A human-animal chimera might be able to."

"Yeah."

"Did the police find any forensic evidence from the killer in the car?"

"Nothing useful. Two fingerprints were found, from two different individuals, and they didn't match any in the database."

"Thanks for calling," I said. "Let's go to Mr. Bokor's office tomorrow."

We said goodnight, and I crawled into bed with my cats lying at my feet.

I'm not as steely as I pretend to be when it comes to horrors. Nightmares about finding Mr. Bokor's body haunted me all night.

I suspected that if we discovered any human-animal chimeras, my future nightmares would be even worse.

CHAPTER 3
THE OFFICE

"Okay." Matt turned from his laptop in the passenger seat of my car. "1-800-Mr-Bokor was registered under the name of Jules Bobideau of Sea Lice Sound. The address appears to be a mail store, though. I did an internet search of his name and came up with a half-dozen people of that name in Sea Lice Sound and Jellyfish Beach."

"Let's ask at his office, then," I said. "It's in one of those shared corporate suites. Maybe his suite mates can give us some info on Mr. Bokor and where he lives."

When we arrived, I recognized the receptionist from my earlier visit here with Madame Tibodet. The woman was a young, pretty Latina who needed to be a skilled actor as she answered the phone and pretended to callers that she worked for each of the various businesses headquartered here. They were, in reality, one-person companies.

The name plate on her desk said her name was Eva Martin.

"Hi, Eva," I said with a fake smile. "We have an appointment with Mr. Bokor."

"He hasn't been in today," the receptionist replied. "He frequently makes on-site consultations."

She clearly hadn't learned yet of Mr. Bokor's demise.

"Oh." I tried to look confused. "I was scheduled for. . ." I glanced at my watch. "Two-thirty."

"I'm sorry. You can wait here." She gestured to the tiny seating area of a loveseat and chair in a minimalist decor.

Matt plopped down on the loveseat and studied his phone.

"Jules even reminded me of the appointment," I said, remaining standing by the front desk.

"Oh, you know his real name?"

"Of course. I've worked with him quite a bit."

"You look familiar. You've been to his office before?"

"Oh, yes. Do you mind if we wait for him in there?"

"I'm sorry. You can't, not when he's not there."

"Okay. It's quite an unusual office, from what I remember."

"I'll say. His incense leaks out from under his door, and it's nasty." She made a face.

"It sure is," said a dorky man who emerged from the nearest office with a sign beside its open door announcing he was a realtor. "I've asked him not to burn it, but he glares at me like he wants me to die. I hesitate to invite clients here because of it."

"Yes, Jules is quite a character," I said.

"He brings his goat to the office," the man added. "We're not supposed to bring pets here."

"Service animals are okay," the receptionist said. "It's his emotional-support goat."

“That’s not a service animal.”

“The goat assists him with his work,” I said. “Like his monkey-cat.”

“His *what*?” asked the realtor.

Matt looked up at me. Oops, I had crossed into dangerous territory.

“He has a cat that looks like a monkey,” I said. “You haven’t seen it?”

The realtor shook his head.

“I’ve seen it,” said a woman’s husky voice from the open door of the next office down the hall, an event-marketing firm. The stocky redhead poked her head out. “It has some bizarre birth defect.”

“I think it’s kind of cute,” the receptionist murmured.

Several offices had their doors open. These people must be lonely in their one-room business empires and were listening to whatever chatter took place in the reception area.

“Have you guys seen any other strange creatures with Mr. Bokor?” I asked.

“He once brought in a squirrel that had reptile scales instead of fur,” said a tall bald guy in the doorway of a personal-injury attorney’s office.

“How do you know it was a squirrel instead of a lizard?” the receptionist asked.

“Because it had a squirrel's head and a fluffy tail.”

“Has anyone seen any strange people visiting him?” I asked.

“Most of the people who visit him are strange,” the redhead said.

“With the exception of you guys,” the receptionist said to me with a smile.

"I mean *really* strange," I said. "Like carnival freaks."

My impromptu focus group thought it over and shook their heads.

"Do you know where Jules lives?" I asked.

"We can't divulge his address," the receptionist said.

"Sea Lice Sound," said the realtor.

"He lives with his brother," the receptionist added.

I thanked them, before asking, "Do you know of anyone who might want to harm Mr. Bokor?"

Silence. It seemed like everyone wore a rueful smile.

"Mr. Bokor makes no effort to be friendly," said the attorney. "We're kind of like a family here, even though we have separate businesses."

"Yeah, and every time you complain about his incense, he burns more just to spite you," said the realtor.

"He takes up two parking spaces with his stupid SUV," said the marketing woman.

"And his goat eats all the landscaping plants by the entrance," added the realtor.

"Why would you ask?" the receptionist asked me.

"Um, I'm worried about why he didn't show up for our appointment."

"It's unprofessional for me to say this," the receptionist went on, "but Jules is a highly disagreeable person. Short-tempered, rude, and domineering. I don't care if he finds out I said that. Like Jeremy said"—she nodded toward the attorney—"we're a family here. There are plenty of companies that would love to lease here, and I'm sure the people would be easier to get along with. That said, I've never heard—from Jules or anyone else—of someone who would want to harm him."

"Good to know," I said. "I feel better now. One last question. Does Mr. Bokor keep any pets in his office overnight?"

"Just the snake in the terrarium," the receptionist said. "Why?"

"If Mr. Bokor doesn't come in over the next couple of days, you might want to feed the snake."

"With what?" the marketer asked.

"A monkey-cat," Matt said.

I scowled at him all the way to the parking lot.

THE ONLY PHONE number on file for Mr. Bokor with the Florida Division of Corporations was 1-800-MR-BOKOR. Calling it gave us only a recorded sales pitch before sending us to voicemail. We had no choice other than to show up at Mr. Bokor's house unannounced.

First, I did some research at home with Matt standing over my shoulder. The realtor having confirmed that the voodoo sorcerer lived in Sea Lice Sound, I searched the property appraiser's website to see if he owned a home there. He did, and he had purchased it this year. It was appraised at an astoundingly high price.

"Who knew that voodoo was so profitable?" I asked Matt.

"He might have come into a lot of money recently, which might explain his murder."

"Possibly. Let's go pay his brother a visit."

"What if he's not home? Should we break in?"

I hesitated. A law-abiding kind of girl, I would rarely

consider breaking and entering. But it was the only way to know for sure if there was one or more human-animal hybrids living in the house.

"We'll see," I replied.

Matt chuckled. "Not the response I would have expected from you. And if his brother *is* there, I doubt he'll let us past the front door."

"True. Let's see how it goes."

I drove north along the interstate for the brief journey to Sea Lice Sound, a charming community that was even smaller than Jellyfish Beach. As you can imagine from their names, the two towns were not named by people with any marketing sense. In fact, their founders were grim, unimaginative fishermen and farmers from the late 1800s. Since then, the town governments never could get it together to change the names.

Mr. Bokor's home was a brand-new, flamboyantly large structure right on the Intracoastal Waterway. The value on the tax appraiser's site was much lower than the multiple millions this place could fetch on the market nowadays.

"I still can't believe a voodoo sorcerer could afford this," I said as we parked in the driveway.

"Maybe he put money in his bank account magically."

"Mrs. Lupis and Mr. Lopez said he also practices alchemy. Maybe he's achieved what alchemists have tried for centuries to do: turn base metals into gold."

"The only honest way I can think of that he could get this wealthy is through his chimeras," Matt said. "Like, someone paid him fantastical amounts of cash for monkey-cats and cat-dogs."

"And human-somethings."

The thought of that kept us silent as we walked up to the extravagant entrance. Matt finally spoke before we reached the range of a doorbell-camera microphone.

"If the brother is here, let me play the bad cop," he said. "You play the empathetic one while you cast your truth-telling spell. Did you bring the ingredients?"

"Yes. I knew I might have to cast the spell, but it always seems unfair to use that on people."

"You might not have any other way to get the information you need. If he's cooperative, maybe you won't have to use it."

"Okay."

"And we don't know if he's been notified about his brother," Matt added. "Let's handle this carefully."

Matt rang the doorbell. The door opened only about two inches, and a young man pressed his face to the gap.

"Yes?"

If this was Mr. Bokor's brother, they certainly weren't twins. The man was Caucasian, while Mr. Bokor was black.

"Are you Jules Bobideau's brother?" Matt asked.

The man snickered. "Jules doesn't have a brother. I'm a friend."

If Jules told his office mates that he lived with his brother, I would hazard a guess that this guy was more than a friend.

"May I ask you some questions about Jules?" Matt asked.

"Whatever for? Did something happen to him?"

No, he hadn't been notified of the death. Matt ran with it.

"Sir, I'm afraid I have news about Jules. May we come in? You'll want to sit down for this."

"Oh, my goodness! Please tell me Jules is okay."

"Let's sit down and talk."

"Do you mind giving me a moment? I'm not properly dressed. Please stay here for a sec."

His face disappeared from the door, but he didn't close it.

Matt and I exchanged glances.

"This is not what I expected," I said.

"Just go with it. While I'm talking with him, excuse yourself to use the bathroom, and snoop around the house."

"That's rude."

"Maybe you'll find a chimera and won't have to use your truth spell."

"Okay," the friend called out from inside the house. "You can come in now."

We walked through a giant foyer. The kitchen was to the left, and Mr. Bokor's friend stood behind the island. We stood opposite him.

"Thank you," Matt said. "I'm Matt Rosen with *The Jellyfish Beach Journal*, and this is Missy Mindle."

"I'm Trevor Fortune."

"Trevor, you'll want to sit down."

"That's okay. I prefer to stand."

"Well, Trevor, um, I regret to inform you that Jules has been murdered."

"No!"

"The police should have notified you by now. It happened last night."

"Someone rang the bell late last night, but I didn't answer it."

Trevor's remaining composure crumbled, and he broke into sobs.

Matt gave me a pointed look.

"Excuse me," I said. "I need to use the bathroom."

With sobs and wails coming from the kitchen, I performed a lightning-fast tour of the house. It was spacious, luxurious, and rather bare. I took issue with Mr. Bokor's uninspired design aesthetic.

Most importantly, no one else was home. No interior doors were locked, and I went into every room. The only chimera I found was the monkey-cat who screeched at me when I peeked into the den where it was sleeping.

When I returned to the kitchen, Trevor was still standing behind the island, his face in his hands. Matt sat at a nearby dining table and studied my face when I entered the room.

I shook my head negatively.

"He was such a great man," Trevor said. "Like a father to me."

"Forgive me for being blunt," Matt said in a soothing voice, "but why would anyone want to kill him?"

"It must have been a robbery gone wrong."

"His wallet wasn't taken. We've learned that Jules was working on a project, and I wonder if that's why someone killed him."

"Project?"

"Using alchemy and magic to create chimeras—hybrid creatures made from different species."

"I don't know what you're talking about."

"Like the monkey-cat," I said.

Trevor glared at me. "That's a cat with a horrible birth defect."

"There's even a rumor about hybrids of humans and

animals," Matt said. "Would you have heard anything about that?"

"You're crazy!"

Matt looked at me and nodded.

I began casting the truth-telling spell. Part of the process involved sprinkling a powder made of several ingredients on or near the subject's feet. I walked toward the island.

"Stay away from me!"

I ducked as a barstool sailed right over my head and crashed into the wall.

Before I could react, Trevor dashed from the kitchen with a clatter of hooves on the tiles.

Yes, that's correct. Hooves.

Below his waist, Trevor had the legs and body of a horse.

Matt and I were frozen, stunned, as the hoofbeats went through the open door from the street and gradually faded away.

"Centaurs," Matt said. "I told you I hated centaurs. They scared the crap out of me when I was a kid. And now, this! I think I'm traumatized."

"You have every right to be."

"Do you think the centaur killed Mr. Bokor? I'll admit that I don't. He seemed convincingly shocked by the news."

"I agree. But there could be other human hybrids out there. Frankly, if I were a freak of nature, I'd want to kill the guy who created me."

"If they're out there, we'd better find them before they kill someone else."

CHAPTER 4
CHIMERA CONUNDRUM

When Matt and I pulled into my driveway, Mrs. Lupis and Mr. Lopez were on my front porch waiting for me. This was highly unusual for them. Normally, they'd time their arrival to occur immediately after I got home.

Perhaps it was our stop at a fast-food restaurant that threw off the timing of my Society handlers.

"Why is there no car parked out front?" Matt asked. "They look like those solicitors who get dropped off in a neighborhood and go from door to door trying to sell you religion or solar panels."

"Yeah, I've never seen a vehicle. And I've never seen them get into a ride-sharing car or a cab. I guess they get beamed here."

Frankly, I suspected that wasn't far from the truth.

We got out of the car, and I waved as I approached my front door.

"Sorry to keep you guys waiting."

"You came into contact with a human-animal chimera?" Mrs. Lupis stated more than asked.

"Tell us all about it," added her partner.

"Let's go inside first," I said, unlocking the door. "Can I get you guys some tea? Beer or wine?" It was early evening, and I had just encountered a centaur. I needed a glass of wine.

"Thank you, but no," Mr. Lopez said.

"Nothing for me," Mrs. Lupis said. "Only your photos of the chimera."

"I didn't take photos."

They couldn't hide their disappointment.

"That's a fundamental responsibility of your job," Mrs. Lupis scolded.

"Look, we expected to find Mr. Bokor's human brother answering the door at their house."

"Who, at first, sounded like more of a friend or someone closer," Matt said.

"We didn't know he was a centaur because he concealed the lower part of his body. We only saw what he was as he galloped out of the home too quickly for me to even get my phone out of my pocket."

The two shook their heads in disappointment.

"Don't you realize how miraculous a sighting that was?" Mrs. Lupis whined. "A centaur, of all creatures."

"Technically, not a true centaur of legend," her partner said. "It was artificially created, after all. Sorry to deflate your childlike joy at discovering the Tooth Fairy actually exists."

"It does exist. Remember, one was documented in Arizona recently."

"That was a crested mouth sprite."

"For all intents and purposes, it was a tooth fairy. Maybe not *the* Tooth Fairy, but a close approximation."

"There's that childlike joy again," Mr. Lopez said with a tight-lipped smile.

"It's why I'm in this field. The wonder of cataloging creatures of legend that shouldn't exist. Isn't it the same for you?"

He smiled more broadly. "I'm certainly not in it for the money."

I was amazed to observe slight traces of personality in my reps from the Society. Perhaps they had become comfortable enough in front of me to let their true selves show. Their weird and robotic true selves.

They returned their attention to me. Unfortunately.

"And you failed to capture documentary evidence," Mrs. Lupis said.

"Sorry. I explained why. Plus, we searched the house and didn't find any other creatures there. But you guys never explained what you ultimately plan to do about the chimeras."

They exchanged uncomfortable glances.

"As is the case with all cryptids, our goal is to catalog and study them," Mr. Lopez said. "Even though these creatures were artificially created."

"Which creates a moral quandary," said Mrs. Lupis.

"What do you mean?"

"These chimeras are technically invasive species. Should they be allowed to exist out in the world where they might harm other, natural creatures? Fortunately, we believe they're not capable of breeding. Also, we do not want the public to become aware of them. That awareness would endanger all legitimate cryptids. If people knew monsters really exist, they would seriously investigate all the things that go bump in the night."

"How many chimeras are out there?" Matt asked. "And is Mr. Bokor the only source of them?"

Mrs. Lupis frowned. I got the feeling she wasn't sure if she could trust Matt.

"We think Mr. Bokor is the only source, at least in this area," Mr. Lopez said. "As to how many are out there, we don't know. We suspect Mr. Bokor was selling them as pets, and we worry that there are several. Ms. Mindle reported seeing two of them herself."

That was correct: the monkey-cat in Mr. Bokor's office and the cat-dog at Igor Stanisloopsky's mansion.

"You never fully answered my question about what you're going to do with them," I said. "Does your 'moral quandary' involve capturing them? Or euthanizing them?"

The partners exchanged pained glances again.

"Capture them," they said in unison.

"And study them," Mrs. Lupis said.

"I don't believe we can, in good conscience, release them afterward," said Mr. Lopez.

"The part-human chimeras especially must stay as our guests. They are the most problematic of all," Mrs. Lupis said.

"You can't keep innocent humans locked away," Matt objected. He was getting himself worked up.

"We believe being only part-human doesn't give them the same rights as humans," Mrs. Lupis said.

"Woah," I said. "This conversation is getting truly disturbing. You have no right to decide who's human and who isn't.

The guy we saw today was one hundred percent human. From the waist up."

"You see why it is such a moral quandary," Mr. Lopez said apologetically. "And why we need to locate all the chimeras."

"I asked, but no one has ruled out euthanasia," I said.

"We would never do that!" both partners insisted.

I wish I was more convinced. In the time since I became a member of the Friends of Cryptids Society of the Americas, I have seen the other members demonstrate only scientific interest and kindness toward cryptids. But my handlers' anxiety over the chimeras alarmed me.

I asked them why they were so concerned.

"It is like the tale of Frankenstein's monster," Mr. Lopez said. "Humans should not play God. Doing so creates disasters."

"As Mr. Bokor learned himself," said Mrs. Lupis. "We believe one of his monsters killed its creator. We don't want it to kill anyone else."

My first impression was that Trevor, the centaur, hadn't killed him. I was confident the monkey-cat hadn't killed him, either. Could there really be other human-animal hybrids out there?

"Your instructions remain the same," Mrs. Lupis said to me. "Find any and all chimeras you can, especially the human ones. And locate the laboratory where Mr. Bokor was creating them."

"Um," Matt raised his hand. "I've seen my share of supernatural phenomena. Some really crazy stuff. But how, exactly, can you create a centaur? It seems impossible."

"We don't know," Mr. Lopez replied. "Obviously, DNA was magically manipulated."

"Obviously," his partner echoed.

"Scientists are doing a lot of gene-editing, leading to tremendous breakthroughs in medicine," Matt said. "But I've never imagined you could combine two different species and make an entirely new one."

"Fortunately, we have a witch on this assignment," Mr. Lopez said, nodding at me. "She can discover how the magic works."

"Angela is more powerful than I am," I said, referring to the Society's enforcer.

"She will play a role in this, for sure."

I hoped her role wouldn't involve killing chimeras.

The partners headed for the front door.

"Enjoy your evening," Mrs. Lupis said. "And let us know when you find the laboratory where the chimeras were created."

After they left, I asked Matt if he had any ideas on how to find the lab.

"No, other than breaking into Mr. Bokor's home and office to look for paperwork, like the lease for a space he could use as a lab. You said he practiced alchemy as well as magic?"

"Yeah."

"Not that I know much about alchemy," he said, "but I assume there's fire, molten metals, caustic chemicals, and stuff like that. His lab would probably be in an industrial park."

This sounded tedious. Being a witch, I trusted intuition a lot, and my gut was telling me there might be an easier route.

"Before we engage in breaking into his house and office, let's begin by covering all our bases," I said.

"Like how?"

"Speak to the one person we know who owns a chimera. I can only assume he got it from Mr. Bokor."

"You mean Igor, the vampire?"

"Yep."

Matt shuddered. "I was afraid you would suggest that."

I studied Matt's face to see if he was truly frightened. No, he wasn't; he was only being dramatic for the humor of it. Admittedly, we had both been intimidated when we visited Igor's over-the-top Transylvania-themed mansion. But we had overcome our fear when it was clear Igor wouldn't attack us.

Matt wasn't a macho guy, but not much scared him. He was a good investigative reporter, and that meant he had plenty of guts. You might say he was a bit overly aggressive to the point of being obnoxious. But that was required to get information from public officials who didn't want to divulge anything.

I felt a warmth in my chest as I gazed at my skinny friend with his shock of unruly hair, his closely cropped beard, and the dimple on his chin. Was I feeling simple admiration, or something more?

Matt noticed me staring at him and gave me his trademark devilish grin.

"You're not scared of Igor," I said. "You just don't like a handsome vampire flirting with me."

"I don't like anyone flirting with you."

"Sorry, but in my forties, I'll take all the flirting I can get."

He smiled again, and all was well in the world.

Until my phone rang. It was Detective Shortle.

"There's been another, uh, Satanic incident."

I was surprised. I had banished the imp who had been

defiling houses of worship for my mother. Had she gotten a new imp?

"Where did it happen?" I asked.

"At the Jellyfish Beach Hotel."

Built along the beach, this hotel was our town's largest. Otherwise, we only had a couple of small inns downtown and a chain motel by the interstate highway. The Jellyfish Beach Hotel was not where I would have expected my mother to strike.

"What was done there?" I asked. "Was it the same ritual used at the houses of worship?"

"No. There was a big, formal event in the ballroom tonight. The attendees reported that the water in goblets at each place setting turned into blood."

"You've got to be kidding me. Actual blood?"

"We're testing it now. The reports said that a horrible sulfur smell filled the room. Then, the doors opened on their own, and a herd of goats rushed in and took food from people's plates."

I stifled a giggle as I imagined the reaction of the well-groomed audience.

"This was while a previously famous music star was singing on the stage," Shortle continued. "Supposedly, bat guano rained down on her."

"How do you know it was bat droppings?"

"Because hundreds of bats flew from above the stage and into the ballroom, getting tangled in the rich people's hair."

I was almost enjoying this story until I reminded myself of the black magic behind it.

"At some point, the fire alarm went off, and people rushed from the room, tripping over the goats. It was a real mess."

"I wonder how they got the goats and bats there?" I mused.

"Don't ask me. You're the one who's an expert in magic."

"I never said I was an expert."

"That's what I call you in my incident reports. That's how I justify consulting with you. Anyway, one more thing allegedly happened. The last of the fleeing attendees reported seeing a giant eyeball floating above the ballroom and the sound of diabolical laughter booming throughout the room."

A sense of dread filled me. The floating eyeball was surely Myron, the demon whom the Knights Simplar wrongly worshipped as an angel. But the other occult activity at the hotel would seem beyond the capability of that cult of doofuses. Only someone like my mother could pull it off.

Either the Knights Simplar had drastically improved their powers, or they were working in league with my mother.

In any event, this posed a big problem for Jellyfish Beach. And for me.

"You never mentioned what this fancy event was for," I said.

"It was a gala—a fundraiser for the Morris Wildlife Sanctuary."

"Why on earth would anyone be hostile to an organization that rescues injured Florida panthers and other critters?"

"I don't know," Shortle said with exasperation. "It makes no sense. I'm going to interview all the directors to see if this is a personal attack against one of them. But my biggest challenge right now is managing how the story gets out to the public."

The sound of frantic clicking made me glance at Matt. He was texting someone, probably because he had learned about the story and was getting it out to the public.

"Just say it was an elaborate prank," I advised. "Say you're investigating who transported the goats and bats there, then released the noxious gas. The blood and the giant eyeball you're going to have to attribute to over-active imaginations."

"My thoughts exactly. Can you come here to the hotel and, uh, see if there was, you know. . ."

"Magic? I can try to sense if there was any. I'll be there soon."

To Shortle, I was no longer a quirky lady working in a botanica. I wondered if she suspected by now that I was an actual witch.

"Can you believe this attack at the Jellyfish Beach Hotel?" Matt asked.

"I'm going there now to meet Detective Shortle. She wants me to sense if magic was used."

"Of course, it was used, and I'm going with you."

"It sounds like the Knights Simplar were involved," I said as we drove toward the beach.

"Why?"

"The giant eyeball floating above the room."

"Oh. I hadn't heard about that."

"Good. I'm glad word isn't spreading about Myron. But I wouldn't be surprised if my mother were involved, too. I know she's forming a black-magic coven in Jellyfish Beach."

"Yeah, that crazy environmentalist, Harriet Chase, is part of it."

"Which is where I get stuck. Why would an environmentalist want to harm a wildlife refuge?"

"Why would the Knights Simplar want to?"

"Shortle thinks it might be a personal attack against a member or members of the board of directors."

Matt grunted. "That's the only explanation that makes sense."

When we arrived at the hotel, the scene was quiet. All the gala attendees had left, and it was late enough that the hotel's guests were settling down for the night. Only two police cars, with their lights off, were parked outside.

"Thanks for coming," Shortle said when we entered the ballroom. She frowned when she saw Matt. "Why are you here, Rosen?"

"I'm a reporter. And you should be grateful I'm here. I'll write a story that covers up the supernatural stuff." He glanced at me. "I've fully compromised my journalistic ethics when it comes to the supernatural. All because of Missy."

"Aren't you cute?" Shortle snarked.

"I see they removed all the animals," I said.

Shortle nodded as Matt and I wandered the room. The wait staff had also removed the goblets of blood from the tables, but the white tablecloths hadn't been removed, and many had blood stains. The air still reeked of sulfur. And the floor was littered with fragments of napkins and food chewed up by the goats.

The floor was also littered with, well, do I really need to say it? The goats had relieved themselves prolifically, as had the bats. The bats had dropped their payloads mostly on the stage, but also across the room.

Aside from the mess, what struck me immediately was the lingering energy of black magic. It made my skin crawl. Elemental magic, the kind I practice, is made with the natural energies of the earth and those of the spell caster. You might leave behind some physical ingredients, such as herbs and powders, if your spell required them. Otherwise, the magic was clean and pure.

Black magic, on the other hand, is foul and corrupt. Much of it requires the assistance of demons or the use of blood sacrifice. Evil is unnatural; it comes from the twisted souls of bad people and the hellish energy of demons.

A witch like me can sense black magic from a mile away. Even normal humans feel uneasy when it's present, though they don't know why.

"Yeah, there was lots of black magic here tonight," I told Shortle.

She studied my face. "You're more than a witchcraft hobbyist, aren't you?"

"I know a thing or two about magic, that's all."

"I don't believe you," she said with a wry smile.

I merely shrugged before telling her goodnight. Enough of demons. It was time to visit a vampire.

CHAPTER 5
SCAM FACTORY

When we had originally met uber-rich Igor Stanisloopsky, he had given me his personal phone number. His doing so drove Matt even deeper into jealousy. But I digress. Calling him at this number, I arranged for Matt and me to pay a visit.

Isolated in a rural part of Crab County, Igor's mansion was the last place you'd want to go at night, especially knowing he was a vampire. His driveway wound through long-leaf pine trees past a small cemetery I hoped was for pets. Then, we came upon the skeletons.

"There were two skeletons hanging from these trees last time we were here," Matt said. "Now, there are seven. These are definitely not Halloween decorations if they've been here for months."

"Maybe he celebrates Halloween year-round."

"Maybe I'll just try not to think about it."

The mansion was an odd morphing of three historical

homes Igor had previously lived in and shipped down to Florida by barge in the late 1800s, when this part of the state was sparsely populated. The Gothic, Victorian, and colonial sections were visually jarring being joined together.

It was unintentionally symbolic of the hybrid species we were investigating today.

At the front door, Igor greeted us warmly with deathly cold handshakes.

"I'm so glad you came to visit," he said with a big smile of brilliantly white teeth, his fangs safely retracted.

As a former home-health nurse for vampires, I'll share a secret. Older vampires need regular teeth-whitening treatments. Human blood tends to stain teeth and not just your fangs.

Matt looked at me to gauge my reactions to Igor. The vampire was probably hundreds of years old, but only in his forties in body age. He was slim, with well-defined pecs and black hair parted on the side. And yes, his skin was quite pale.

"Thank you for being so gracious when we invited ourselves to your home," I said. "We promise we won't take up much of your time."

"Worry not. I have an eternity to spend. So, you mentioned you had questions about Nelly."

"Your cat-dog? Yes, we do. Did you get her from Mr. Bokor?"

"I did. Nelly was made to order by poor Mr. Bokor. I've been so distressed to hear he was murdered. We had a recent falling out of sorts, but it doesn't mean I grieve for him any less."

"You guys weren't getting along?" Matt asked.

Igor chuckled. "Indeed. That makes me a suspect in his murder, doesn't it?"

Matt didn't answer. You don't want to get a vampire mad at you.

"Did Mr. Bokor create other chimeras like your pet?" I asked, changing the subject.

"Chimera is such an exotic word. I just call them hybrids. And yes, he created several of them to sell to the very wealthy who wanted unique pets. A highly profitable enterprise. Especially since hybrids can't reproduce. Every new one had to be created by Mr. Bokor."

That explained how Mr. Bokor could afford his lavish home.

"How did Mr. Bokor's magic work?" Matt asked. "He didn't just cast a spell and turn a dog's head into a cat's head, right?"

I was the one who was supposed to be asking the questions about magic, but I allowed Igor to answer.

"Of course not." He chuckled. "Even voodoo isn't that powerful. I'll explain it the best I can, not being magical myself. To create Nelly, Mr. Bokor secured a pregnant cat and dog who were at the same stage of gestation. He made them drink a strange-looking potion that the animals couldn't resist. Next, he tied the two pregnant mothers together, with their abdomens touching. Finally, he conducted a lengthy voodoo ceremony that he told me was his own invention."

"That's it?" I asked.

"Yes. After the normal number of weeks, the dog and the cat each gave birth. The cat produced a cat-dog, with the head of a cat and the body of a dog. The dog produced a dog-cat, with the opposite: the head of a dog and body of a cat."

"No medical procedures?" Matt asked. "No gene editing?"

"No. To the observer, like me, it appeared very simple.

Though, I doubt any other magician could achieve such a feat." He gave me a piercing stare. "How advanced in witchcraft are you, my dear?"

"How did you know I'm a witch?"

"Like you, we vampires can sense the supernatural in others."

"I'm nowhere near advanced enough to make chimeras. In fact, I suspect it requires black magic."

"It very well might. But, you know, whatever it takes to make a lucrative product is okay with me."

I wasn't surprised he said that. Vampires are notoriously amoral.

"Now, while creating hybrids of less-advanced animals seemed easy to me, we found making human hybrids almost impossible."

"Wait, did you say *we*?"

"Yes. I wasn't just a customer of Mr. Bokor's, I was his partner. I had sufficient resources to bankroll him until we made a profit. We could have gone on raking in the bucks forever, but I had to complicate matters. I wanted to make human hybrids."

"Um, why?" Matt asked.

"I'll show you why. Follow me."

He led the way through a maze of hallways, taking us on a journey of architectural history as we passed through each section of the cobbled-together house. We'd followed this path before, so I wasn't surprised when we entered the giant garage-like structure that housed dozens of cubicles.

I was surprised, however, to find it empty.

"Yes, my scam slaves are gone," he said proudly. "I demonstrated my bountiful generosity by releasing them from the spell that had mesmerized them."

"How kind of you," Matt muttered.

"It was, wasn't it? But how can I run a scam factory without enslaved workers? In places like Cambodia, they lure workers with false promises of well-paying jobs, then they imprison them. They're forced to work long hours fooling people through text messages, emails, and phone calls into parting with their money. But I only enslaved evil people: the dirtbags who ran such operations here in Florida."

"You took the moral high ground," Matt said.

"Absolutely." Clearly, Igor wasn't hearing Matt's sarcasm. "But look at me now. I have no workers. That's why Mr. Bokor and I were trying to create the ideal scammer: an intelligent human coupled with an elephant."

"Why an elephant?" I asked.

"Because they only need a couple of hours of sleep each night. Think of how many more hours a day the hybrids could work than normal humans."

"But it takes so much longer for a human hybrid to develop than a pet."

"I'm immortal," Igor replied. "I didn't mind waiting for my new slaves to grow old enough to work. The technology and scams evolve over the years, but we'd just use the new ones. The scam industry always adapts and will thrive until the end of time."

I felt dizzy from the twisted, debased evil of this scheme.

"What was the deal with the centaur?" Matt asked.

"Oh, you saw him? Mr. Bokor just thought it would be cool to have one as a companion. I don't know why."

Before my brain exploded, I tried to focus on our mission.

"Where is the lab where Mr. Bokor performed his magic?" I asked.

"It's here in my home. Follow me."

We returned to the main house and went down an unfamiliar corridor of the Victorian portion of the structure. It ended at an elevator, an old-fashioned type with a folding steel gate inside of the sliding door. Matt and I followed Igor inside, and the machine clanked and rattled up to the third floor.

"Here we are," Igor said, manually opening the door and gate.

We stepped out into a large room with polished oak floors and steel rafters. At first, it looked more like a Victorian-era kitchen than a lab, with zinc counters, a cast-iron stove, and long shelves with beakers and flasks.

At the far end of the room, it had the feel of a veterinarian's office with two large steel tables placed side by side.

"How many human hybrids were created?" I asked.

"Aside from the centaur, there's a human-elephant hybrid."

I hissed involuntarily from shock. "Where is it?"

"Alas, he escaped. The elephant hybrids were meant to be mostly human, but this one turned out with too much elephant in him, and he went on a stampede about a couple of weeks ago. I don't know where he went."

"Oh, my. This is a mess," I said.

"It sure is. I have lost two major sources of income: my scam factory and the exotic pet business. That's why I agreed to see you two tonight. I want to punish whoever murdered Mr. Bokor."

"Why do you think we can find the murderer?" I asked.

"Because you successfully solved the murder of my financial manager. And because you have ties to those who I suspect are guilty."

"Who?"

"The Friends of Cryptids Society. I know all about them. I'm certain they killed Mr. Bokor to stop him from making hybrids."

I gasped.

"Why are you so surprised?" Igor looked at me through squinted eyes. "You work for them. Mr. Bokor told me that."

"The Society is very secretive," I said, in denial of Igor's accusation.

"Word gets around in the supernatural community when humans—and non-humans—poke around in our affairs."

"Non-humans?" Who was he referring to? Mrs. Lupis and Mr. Lopez?

He ignored my question. "They care little about me because vampires are so common. Ho-hum. My kind was cataloged by the Society centuries ago. They're more interested in finding new cryptids and other exotic entities. The hybrids—or chimeras, as you call them—must drive the Society members crazy."

"But that would never be a reason for them to murder someone."

He arched his eyebrows. "Oh, and you're privy to all their motives and activities?"

"No, but—"

"Did you know they requested an interview with Mr. Bokor? He turned them down, of course."

"When was this?"

"Less than a month before his death."

"Do you have any proof to back up your accusation?" Matt asked.

Igor calmly regarded him through eyes that were slitted once more. He hissed.

Matt jumped in a panic.

The vampire laughed. "I wouldn't share any proof with you, Mr. Newspaperman. I shall use it when I'm ready and take down the entire organization, if necessary."

My gut told me he was bluffing and didn't have any proof. But I wouldn't bet anything on my gut being correct.

"I'm sorry that you lost your business partner," I said. "And when we find the true murderer, you'll see that your accusation is wrong. In the meantime, if you find out where the escaped human hybrids are, please let me know."

"So, you can tell the Society? Why should I help them kill those poor creatures?"

"Those creatures will probably be killed by random humans with guns. I want to prevent that. The Society assured me the creatures will be treated well."

"You may believe them, but don't expect me to."

"Thank you for your time, Mr. Stanisloopsky. Um, I'm not sure I remember how to reach the front door."

He let us out through a heavily armored side door of the garage, built to keep his former slaves from escaping should their mesmerization wear off. That was before he freed them. I didn't know why he did, but I doubted it was because of altruism.

Matt remained silent until we were rolling down the winding driveway.

"Do you think he really suspects the Society?" Matt asked.

"I don't know, but I'm almost certain he has no evidence."

"I agree. In fact, he might be tossing us a red herring, so we won't suspect him."

"You think Igor murdered him?"

"He's a more likely suspect than someone from the Society. Maybe they had a falling out over money."

"If Igor did it, he wouldn't have cut Mr. Bokor's throat and wasted all that tasty blood."

"He would have if he wanted it to look like someone other than a vampire did it."

I hoped Matt was right. Thinking about the Society, the person most likely to be assigned to kill Mr. Bokor would be Angela, the enforcer. But I simply couldn't imagine the sweet, elderly mage would kill anything other than a violent monster.

The Society had ordered me to locate the chimeras. But now, I realized I needed to solve the murder, as well. It was the only way I would know for sure that Angela and others at the Society were innocent.

If they weren't, I couldn't in good conscience work with them anymore. Even if that meant losing all the money they had given me.

CHAPTER 6
TOUGH DAYS AHEAD

I visited Angela on my own without inviting Matt along. This needed to stay within the Society's family, for now. If I discovered they were responsible for the murder, well, then they would have to answer to the authorities of the outside world.

My visit was especially delicate because Angela was a friend and my new mentor in magic. Aside from being a powerful mage, she was relatively normal, at least compared to Mrs. Lupis and Mr. Lopez. They would never give me honest answers like Angela would.

However, if the Society had murdered Mr. Bokor, it would have been most likely at the hands of Angela because she was the local enforcer. Awkward!

She had told me to stop by after dinner and look for her in her backyard. That was where I found her, arranging a dozen pumpkins on the ground near the swimming pool of this property that was much too luxurious for someone on a librarian's salary.

The pumpkins had faces drawn on them with black marker. The faces were realistic, not like typical Jack-o'-lanterns. I figured she was going to carve them back here, and then bring them to the front yard as Halloween approached.

"Nice pumpkins," I said. "Such realistic-looking faces. I didn't realize you had an artist in you."

She laughed. "I have many talents, I guess. What did you want to chat about?"

"You heard about the voodoo sorcerer who was murdered?"

"Of course I did. Everyone in the supernatural community is talking about it. And the Society is upset about the chimeras he created."

"Yes. They told me they were not happy about them."

"For good reason. We mortals should never play God and create creatures that weren't meant to exist."

"I suppose," I said, "the bokor needed to be stopped."

"Would you be so kind to step away from the pumpkins, dear?"

Angela motioned for me to move to the side of the yard while she faced the pumpkins from twenty feet away.

I tried to phrase my question carefully.

"Do you believe the sorcerer—"

Blue lightning shot from Angela's right hand and the pumpkin furthest from me exploded.

"Sorry to startle you," Angela said. "I've been lax about getting regular target practice."

"Um, no worries. I was just asking if—"

Another bolt of lightning hit a pumpkin in the middle of the row, blasting to pieces its uncannily realistic human face. Orange goop and pumpkin seeds rained upon the lawn.

"You were saying, dear?"

"I'll wait until you're finished."

Angela blew up the pumpkins one by one from different positions: standing, crouching, lying prone. She took her last shot while diving like an action-movie heroine.

Every bolt of blue lightning hit its intended target with perfect accuracy. Every pumpkin was obliterated.

"I'm going to collect the seeds, wash them, and toast them with salt. Delicious for snacking," she said, smiling proudly.

"Aren't you concerned about your neighbors?"

"They can't see much through the hedges. I just tell them I'm firing an AR-15 with a silencer, and they're fine with that."

"Of course." I shook my head. I was finding it less difficult to believe Angela was capable of whacking Mr. Bokor.

"I'll let you get back to what you were asking me," she said as she bent over, scooping up pumpkin guts from her pool patio.

"How far would the Society go to stop Mr. Bokor from making chimeras?"

"We sent him a letter requesting an interview. Had he complied, we would have been quite adamant in insisting he stop."

"Exactly how adamant?"

"If we needed to raise our voices, we would have."

"Raised voices. That's all? What about threats?"

"There is no magic guild in Jellyfish Beach or any part of Crab County. There's no one with the authority to *make* someone stop."

"But you agree he needed to be stopped?"

"Absolutely. What he was doing was morally wrong, and it endangered true cryptids."

"So, how would you stop him, other than raising your voices?"

She stood straight and frowned at me.

"Are you implying we harmed that man?"

"To be honest, I'm not implying. I'm asking."

"Missy, you know full well that our focus is on scientific research and the preservation of monsters. We're not monsters ourselves."

"Please don't take this personally, but you're an enforcer. Aren't you supposed to, um, get rid of troublesome creatures?"

"Come inside, and let's talk."

I followed her into her kitchen. Had I pushed her too far? Was this where I would die?

She opened a cabinet and pulled out a bottle of expensive Scotch, splashing it into two glasses and handing one to me.

"Sit down," she commanded as she sat at the kitchen table, piercing me with her stare.

I sat across from her. "I don't drink Scotch."

"It's one of the finest made. You'll drink it and enjoy it."

It burned my nose just sniffing it. I took a sip and grimaced, though it was smooth and smoky. I had to admit it relaxed me a bit.

"I've never killed a human in my life," Angela said, giving me a stern look. It was the look she gave noisy children in the library, dialed up to eleven.

"I've killed invasive pythons in the Everglades," she continued, "because they were wiping out the population of chupacabras. I killed a shark that was attacking a mermaid. The only cryptid I've killed was a psychotic troll who was feeding on humans so carelessly he would have been captured by the police. When I attempted to transport him to another environment, he almost ate me. What enforcers do is capture cryptids for study and release. And relocate troublemakers."

I took another sip of scotch. Actually, it was a gulp.

"I never meant to accuse you," I said in a scratchy voice. "Could another enforcer, or someone else in the Society, have killed him?"

"Why are you so focused on the Society? I'm sure a rogue sorcerer like Mr. Bokor had many enemies who could have killed him."

"Someone told me they thought the Society was responsible."

"Who?"

"I'm not at liberty to say."

"You are a member of the Friends of Cryptids Society. Why are you taking the side of some individual against us?"

She had a point. Guilt spread through me as I wondered how I had allowed a Machiavellian vampire to make me doubt my benefactors so easily.

"Igor Stanisloopsky," I said. "He was Mr. Bokor's partner in making the chimeras."

Angela took a long swallow of scotch and shook her head sadly.

"You take the word of a morally challenged vampire who was financially entwined with the victim?"

"You know him?"

"I'm not friends with lots of vampires like you are, Missy, but I do know about the wealthiest person in Jellyfish Beach."

I nodded.

"Actually, I think the Society hit him up for donations, and he turned us down," she said with a smile.

"I'm sorry for seeming disloyal. When he accused the Society, it was so unexpected and such a horrifying thought that I had to make sure it was false. You must understand that Mrs. Lupis and Mr. Lopez had just ordered me to look for chimeras. They were very upset about the human hybrids."

"Yes, I heard about them. Very disturbing. How much human do they have in them?"

"There are supposedly only two of them. I've only seen one, and he was a centaur. So that means he's half human?"

"Centaurs have human hands, you realize."

"Yeah."

"Hands that can use a blade to murder someone."

I got the point. Members of the Society were the least likely culprits, especially compared to an amoral business partner and two Frankenstein monsters.

"Again, I'm sorry," I said. "And for wasting your time, too."

"Not at all. Have some more scotch."

"It's not really my kind of drink."

"Nonsense." She poured me half a glass. "Drink up. You have tough days ahead."

"Business partners squabble all the time," Matt said as my car turned onto Mr. Bokor's street.

"If Igor killed him, it had to be over something big. Even if Mr. Bokor stole money from him, Igor's so rich, he'd really have to lose a lot to be sent over the edge. I'm hoping to find evidence of another business they had together. Or maybe, there's an additional personal connection we don't know about. I also want to see if we can learn more about the human hybrids."

"Dang. There's crime-scene tape across the door. I guess the cops are still combing the house for evidence. We'll have to come back another time."

I pulled into the driveway and parked.

"We don't have time. Even if there's nothing here pointing to the murderer, we need help in finding the chimeras."

"*We?* I'm just helping you out."

"You never let me down." I opened my door. "And I know you won't with this."

"Wait a minute. I've crossed the line too often as a reporter, but trespassing on a crime scene is something you just don't do."

"It's not a crime scene. And we won't disturb any forensic evidence."

"How do you know we won't?"

I shrugged. "Let's go. Move with confidence so the neighbors will think we're supposed to be here."

I got out and closed my door before he could protest further.

When I reached the front door, I cut the yellow tape. I would reattach it with a spell on our way out. Matt joined me by the time my unlocking spell was cast, and the deadbolt clicked open.

"I can't believe we're doing this," Matt said under his breath.

I led the way inside. There was a lingering smell of horse dung I hadn't noticed when we were here last. The centaur's doing, no doubt.

In the kitchen, there were traces of fingerprinting dust on the cutlery drawers. I saw no other signs that the police had been in here.

I walked through the house slowly. Last time we were here, while Matt distracted the centaur, I raced through the place looking only for chimeras. Now, I searched more carefully—without touching anything—passing through the family room with a gigantic TV and the palatial living room. The furniture was sparse, and the home didn't truly look lived in.

"I found the centaur's room," Matt called from down the hall.

A bedroom had been partially converted into a stable. Half walls created a stall in the corner with tile on the floor topped with hay. The rest of the room looked like it was used by a human, though, with a standing desk, a dresser, and a moderately sized TV on the wall.

"It looks like the centaur lived here full-time," Matt said. "I guess Mr. Bokor treated him like a son. I feel bad that we chased him away."

"Better that than the police finding him."

"True."

We continued from room to room. The master bedroom and bath were larger than my entire house, but again, were almost empty of possessions. Furniture was limited to a bed, dresser, and chair. The closet contained very little clothing. It was all modern, casual wear—no ritual voodoo garb. The bathroom was sparkling clean with only minimal personal-care articles.

"Mr. Bokor must have spent very little time here," Matt said. "I went back to the property appraiser's site. He's owned it for four years, but you wouldn't know it by looking around."

"Did he build it?"

"I think so. The first owner listed on the property bought it forty years ago. And Mr. Bokor bought it for a pittance. He must have knocked down the old place and built this."

We continued our tour. There were no signs of chimeras, or even normal pets. No voodoo paraphernalia, either. The place was as soulless as Mr. Bokor apparently was.

We came upon an office, which held only a desk and a printer beside stacks of papers. They were real estate listings.

"I wonder if he was into flipping houses," I said. "He didn't seem the type who would do the renovations himself, but he could have done the buying and selling."

"He obviously had a lot of cash on hand. Did it all come from selling chimeras and from Igor?"

"Good question. I think we should pay a visit to the office he rented. Maybe the folks there know if he was heavily into real estate."

"If Mr. Bokor was running a business flipping houses, could that have caused a conflict with Igor?" Matt asked.

"I don't see why it would. Unless he got too busy in real estate and wasn't working hard enough to create hybrid slaves for Igor. We'll need to learn more."

A series of crashes came from the direction of the garage. Matt and I exchanged glances, then rushed toward the noise.

I opened the interior door to the four-car garage to find no vehicles inside it, only a couple of piles of boxes. The aluminum automatic door at the far left had been wrenched open enough to allow a person to enter. No person was in the garage right now.

"Oh, my," was all I could say.

No, it wasn't a person. It was a human-animal hybrid—the elephant-human we had heard about.

And the creation of this chimera had not gone well.

CHAPTER 7
HYBRID HORROR

If you've read a book or seen the movie about the historical Englishman called the Elephant Man, get his image out of your mind. This creature was nothing like him.

This was a young man of large stature but of normal proportions, wearing shorts and a T-shirt with the image of a famous cartoon mouse. He wore no shoes because he had the feet of an elephant. Literally.

His skin was the gray, wrinkled skin of a pachyderm. His hands were normal human hands, aside from the skin. They would be capable of operating a computer keyboard or a smartphone to perpetrate financial scams.

And they could handle an ice pick or similar weapon.

His face was human-sized. In fact, he wore a baseball cap. But the face had the same elephant skin as the rest of him. And there were other glaring differences from normal human physiology.

Yes, you guessed it. He had giant, flapping elephant ears. And his nose was a trunk that hung down to his chest.

"What are you looking at?" he asked us.

"Just wondering what the noise was out here," I said.

"I came here to look for my dad," the elephant hybrid said.

"Why didn't you just come in through the house?" Matt asked.

"Because a strange car is parked out front. And there's crime-scene tape hanging from the front door. A couple of these boxes are mine. One of them has my collection of baseball cards. I found a guy who will buy them."

"Where have you been staying?" I asked.

"I ran away from home a while ago, and I took one of Dad's credit cards. I've been chilling at the Slumber Suites, ordering everything I need with apps."

With no warning, his nose curled upwards, and he trumpeted like an elephant. It appeared to be a nervous tic.

"I don't enjoy going out in public," he added. "Did something bad happen here? Where is Dad?"

My brain snapped out of its stunned condition, and I quickly cast a sleep spell.

I forgot that elephants rarely sleep.

"Why am I feeling all weird?" he cried. "What are you doing to me?"

He charged us like a bull elephant, thankfully one without tusks.

Matt pushed me back inside the house and took the brunt of the collision, crashing backward into the drywall.

It was too late for a protection spell because the chimera was already in contact with us. So, I quickly went through the steps of my immobility spell, grasping the power charm in my pocket for extra strength.

The chimera wrapped his trunk around Matt's neck and yanked him forward, punching him in the stomach. Matt grunted with each blow.

I quickly recited the Latin words, feeling the energy leave my solar plexus and fly from my body. The chimera tossed Matt aside and came for me.

Until he froze like a statue. His eyes bore into me with anger.

My hands were shaking so much I could barely operate my phone.

"Angela," I said, "I caught one of them. Please bring a crew here quickly before my immobility spell wears off."

"What kind of chimera?" she asked.

"Human-elephant."

"Amazing! Send me your location, and we'll be right there."

I fed more energy into my spell to make sure it held. I also sprinkled my special powder on his face and trunk as I cast my truth-telling spell.

"What is your name?" I asked him.

"Pete."

"Why did you run away from home?"

"I wanted to see the world. I was tired of being locked up in the house. Dad said I was special—different from other boys—and people would be afraid of me. But I wanted some adventure."

"How did your adventure go?"

"Dad was right. People were freaked out. I had to tell them I was wearing my Halloween costume early. Then, like I told you, I holed up in a hotel."

"Pete, I command you to tell the truth. Did you kill your dad, Jules Bobideau?"

"No. Why would I do that? Are you saying Dad is dead? Where is he?"

He began crying. It included honking noises through his trunk that were pretty awkward to hear.

I'm not a hard-nosed detective, and thus I'm probably gullible, but I believed him thanks to my truth-telling spell. Plus, he appeared to have no motive to kill Mr. Bokor, and my witchy senses recognized the truth in his voice.

Holding my power charm in my left hand and placing my right on Pete's shoulder, I pulsed soothing magic into his system, temporarily easing his sorrow. It wasn't a spell; it was simply my empathy turned into psychic energy.

Matt lay crumpled on the garage floor, groaning and wheezing. The wind had been knocked out of him by the punches.

"Should I call an ambulance?" I asked.

He shook his head and got onto all fours, his breathing sounding better now.

He reached into the open box in front of him and pulled out a baseball card.

"A 1954 Mickey Mantle! Do you realize how much this is worth?"

"Enough to pry open a garage door to get it, evidently."

Angela arrived more quickly than I had expected. Even more surprising was the arrival of an unmarked black panel van. I pressed the button that opened the garage doors on the left, and the van parked inside. Two attendants from the Society popped out. I recognized the guys from a recent extraction of South American ogres.

"How did you get here so quickly?" I asked.

"We always have crews on standby. Speed is of the essence with cryptids who might be seen in public."

Angela studied Pete who was, thankfully, still immobile. She uttered a spell silently and passed her palm over the creature's face. His eyes closed peacefully.

"That should sedate him," she said.

"My sleep spell didn't work," I explained lamely to the more powerful mage.

"This creature is amazing. I can't imagine how powerful the magic had to be to create him. Too bad it was evil magic."

"He seems to be in good health. Unfortunately, I told him about his dad's passing, though."

"Dad?"

"That's what he called Mr. Bokor. I guess 'adoptive dad' is the accurate term. I wonder if he knows he has two mothers?"

Angela rubbed her eyes. "This is simply too weird."

The attendants carefully wrapped the chimera in moving blankets and put him inside the van.

"What are you going to do with him?" I asked.

"We'll study and debrief him carefully. Then, we'll take him to a safe place where he can live happily in comfort. Don't you dare accuse us of harming him."

"Never again," I promised.

"Someday, we'll take you to the cryptid sanctuary so you can see how well we care for the ones who can't be released back into the wild. You'll be pleasantly surprised."

It was ironic that she was talking about a cryptid sanctuary when my mother was behind disrupting a fundraiser for an animal sanctuary.

I wish there was a sanctuary for tired, old witches like me.

Our tangling with an elephant-man made me look forward to a relaxing evening. After feeding the cats and my iguana witch's familiar, I would have a glass of wine, a simple meal, and a long bubble bath.

I felt weak after my adrenaline had faded away, and I entered my darkened house only half awake. Big mistake.

Right after I closed the front door behind me and walked through the foyer, I was ambushed. Two men wearing masks sprang from the dining room and grabbed my arms. A third man, behind me, shoved a rag in my mouth and pulled a pillowcase over my head. Someone bound my wrists with a painfully tight zip tie.

This was not the best way to realize I should have set wards to protect the house when I left today.

I screamed, but it was muffled by the rag.

"We're going on a little trip, witch."

I recognized the voice instantly. It was Tim Tissy, who preferred to go by the moniker Lord Arseton of the Knights Simplar. Would these clowns forever be a thorn in my side?

I'd been lulled into complacency because of their buffoonery, but they were still thugs who had almost killed Matt once.

The original two men yanked me through the house. Though I was blinded by the pillowcase, I sensed we were passing through the kitchen, then out the back door.

I struggled to think of a spell for fighting back. Most of my go-to spells, such as the immobility one, require me to see my target. Since they had already seized me, it was too late for a protection spell to be effective.

The rumble of a car engine came from my driveway. My captors pulled me, stumbling, around the side of the garage toward the driveway.

Aha! A spell came to mind! A simple one that created and amplified normal static electricity. I quickly worked on it, gathering my internal energies to power the spell while I was dragged toward the car.

The spell engaged. The entire surface of my body crackled with static electricity, harmless to me.

Both men howled with pain and released my arms.

Harmless to me, but not to anyone touching me.

But before I could run, I was shoved hard into the car, landing on the floor behind the front seat. The door slammed shut. The door on the other side opened, and someone got into the back seat and held my neck to the floor with his foot.

He wore boots with rubber soles, impervious to being shocked by my spell.

The front passenger door opened and closed. And the car took off.

Missy are you in danger? asked a New-York-accented voice in my head. It was my telepathic iguana.

Yes, Tony. You're a little late in noticing.

This weather makes me sluggish. I'm cold-blooded, remember?

I explained my predicament and asked for suggestions for magic I could use, given my being blindfolded, gagged, and bound in the back of a car.

A fog spell. It will make the car impossible to drive.

We're already driving.

Cast it when the car stops at a light. Do you know how?

Yeah. I had planned to use it when I took my bath tonight to create a sauna effect. The best-laid plans.

Like my previous spell, this one was also simple. I didn't have to look at anyone, make any hand movements, or recite an incantation out loud. When I felt the car stop, I merely gathered my energies, did the incantation in my head, and sent my energy throughout the car's interior.

It vaporized the humidity in the air, turning it into fog. I couldn't see it but felt it on my skin.

"What the heck?" asked a male voice. "What's wrong with your car?"

"It must be the witch's doing," said Lord Arseton.

"Open the windows."

A horn honked behind us.

"The light must have turned green. We can't be late."

The car lurched ahead.

"Can you see anything?"

"I'm sticking my head out the window," said Lord Arseton. "We're only a couple of blocks—"

I slammed into the back of the seat in front of me amid a crunch of metal and breaking glass. The guy whose boot was on my neck was now lying on top of me. Groaning came from the front seat.

My body hurt from the man landing on me, but I didn't believe I was injured.

"Come on, we have to get the witch to Saint Ruth," said Lord Arseton. "Let's get out of here before the cops show up. We'll just walk the rest of the way."

The rear door opened.

"Get off her, you idiot."

The man pushed himself off me, which hurt even more, and two pairs of hands pulled me out of the car.

"Let's go," said Lord Arseton.

"What about Rick?"

"He'll be fine. He can stay here and take the blame for the crash."

The two men roughly dragged me along the street. I almost tripped on the curb as they stepped onto the sidewalk.

It must have been quite a sight: two men walking a bound captive with a pillowcase over her head through the streets of Jellyfish Beach. You'd think the police, or someone out walking their dog, would rescue me. But in this town, the police are incompetent, and most of the residents are already in bed at this hour.

Now, I had to stumble up concrete steps. A doorbell buzzed.

"Yes?" asked a woman's raspy voice over an intercom. The voice was familiar.

Too familiar.

CHAPTER 8
I'M NOT A JOINER

The door buzzed, and one of my captors pushed it open. We walked along a tiled floor. An elevator dinged, and I was pulled inside.

I heard the front door we had just come through open.

"Hold the elevator, please," called an elderly male voice.

Footsteps approached along with the squeaky wheels of a walker. Lord Arseton cursed under his breath.

"Thank you," said the old man. "What's wrong with your friend?"

"She just had plastic surgery to fix a really ugly nose," Arseton said. "She doesn't want to be seen in public until it heals."

"Ah, vanity," the old man said.

I cried out for help, but with my gag, it came out as "ugh-ee!"

"She also had dental surgery today," Arseton said.

"Wow, this has not been an easy day for her," the clueless man replied.

Talk about the understatement of the year.

The man got out on the next floor. We went up one more level before I was pushed out of the elevator and dragged a short distance. Someone knocked on a door, and it squeaked open. I was pushed inside.

"It's been such a long time since I've seen you, dearie," said the raspy voice I'd heard on the intercom.

It was my mother's.

Someone behind me pulled the pillowcase from my head, and I beheld the monster who had birthed me, then put me up for adoption.

The air in the apartment reeked of sulfur, an unidentifiable noxious incense, and cigarette smoke.

"Behold Saint Ruth," Lord Arseton said, removing my gag. "Bow before her."

How anyone could call this woman a saint was beyond me. Besides, there already was a Saint Ruth.

"I will not bow to my mother," I said. My tongue felt like concrete.

"*Mother?*" asked the goon who came with Arseton.

I took in my surroundings. We were in the living room of an apartment with furniture pushed to the walls and a large circle drawn with chalk surrounding an inverted pentagram on the hardwood floor. Black candles burned at each of the five points of the star, and a copper bowl of incense smoked in the center.

Three women wearing black robes knelt on the other side of the circle. I recognized one as Harriet Chase, the founder of a radical environmental group that went by its acronym, NUTS.

My mother faced me on this side of the circle. Ophelia Lawthorne, who used the alias Ruth Bent, had aged very little since I had last seen her. Her short black hair was speckled with a little more gray than before, and her face was a bit more weathered, probably from all the cigarettes like the one stuck in the side of her mouth. Her high cheekbones were more pronounced from weight loss, and her once pert nose was more rounded now.

I saw traces of myself in her. And an evil that I had, thankfully, not inherited.

"Yes, I gave birth to this woman," my mother replied to the goon. "But I didn't raise her. If I had, she'd be much more powerful than the kitchen witch she is."

"You're the daughter of a saint?" Arseton asked me. "Why didn't you tell us?"

"She's not a saint. And that eyeball you think is an angel is actually a demon. Now, can you cut off this zip tie? My hands have gone numb."

"She *is* a saint," he said as he complied with my request. "We've seen her perform miracles."

"Don't you have to be dead to be declared a saint?"

"No," Ruth said. "I'm self-declared. And my miracles are the proof of my sainthood."

"Your miracles are black-magic spells."

"Don't play word games. Aren't you wondering why you were brought here tonight?"

"I assume you plan to kill me. After all, you've tried before."

She cackled with a sound like an ancient coffin opening. The cigarette bobbled on her lips.

"It was nothing personal, dearie. You were interfering with my work, and I needed to get you out of the way."

"Oh, that makes me feel much better."

"And why would I kill you after you so kindly healed my kidneys with your magic?"

I shrugged. "Because you're evil?"

She smiled. "Finally, you understand. I do admit I partly blame you for my magic being neutralized by the Magic Guild. Fortunately, I grew it back."

"Congratulations. Now, what do you want with me?"

"I want you to join my coven, my followers." She gestured to the others in the room.

"No thanks. I'm not much of a joiner."

"Don't you want to worship your own mother?" Arseton asked.

"Not if it means I'm on the same team as you, dimwit."

"Now, now. The Knights Simplar are a valuable part of my followers," Ruth said. "Once I convinced the Angel Myron to obey me, the Knights gladly joined the fold."

"You used your magic to enthrall the demon?"

She nodded almost imperceptibly.

"Were you behind the defilements of churches and other houses of worship?"

"I sure was," she said proudly. "Stealing souls is a great power booster."

"You still haven't explained what you're doing here in Jellyfish Beach."

She placed her hand on the small of my back and led me into the tiny kitchen. I was taller than she, and her late-seventy-year-old's body was thin, but she radiated strength and power. I believed part of it was inherent, and the rest of it came from her magic.

"I'm changing my business model," she said in a voice low enough that the others wouldn't hear.

A smelly pot of what looked like entrails bubbled on the stove.

"How so?"

"Ever since I went off on my own, I've made a living as a sorceress for hire, causing death and ruin at the will of the highest bidder. When I got gigs with lobbyists in the state capital, the money rolled in. But most of the time, I only got small jobs. You know, make a cheating husband's privates wither away or cause a rival's business to fail. Stuff like that. And my clients were cheap. Those days are finally gone."

"Have you saved enough to retire?"

"Absolutely not. That's why I changed my business model. Today, I operate on a subscription basis."

"What are you talking about?"

"All my followers pay me dues. You can call them tithes, like the Knights Simplar prefer to do. The more followers I have, the more money I make. All I need to do is perform a miracle now and then for followers who pray hard enough for me. That's why I'm building a coven in Jellyfish Beach, connected to those I have in other places."

"You have other covens?"

"Across half the state." She beamed. "Now, I'm a mother you can be proud of."

"For sure." I didn't hide my sarcasm. "By the way, were you involved in disrupting a gala for the Morris Wildlife Sanctuary?"

She chuckled. "That's what I mean by performing miracles. Turning water into blood!"

"Why were you harassing them? They're a good cause."

"The Knights Simplar prayed for me to attack them."

"But why?"

"They believe animal shifters live there." She twirled a finger around her ear. "The Knights Simplar are a little kooky, but I love them anyway."

I already had enough on my plate now but figured I should check out what was going on with the sanctuary. I didn't want the Knights Simplar to mess up their operations.

"You or Lord Arseton better not harm any animals."

"No animals. But maybe a shifter if there really is one at the sanctuary."

"Look, I'm sorry, but I won't be joining your coven. I'm too busy at the botanica I co-own. Plus, I still do some home-health nursing for a few clients."

"I won't take much of your time."

"I don't want to pay dues to you."

"Haven't you come into some money? That's what I heard."

"It all went into the botanica. Besides, I don't want to be involved with black magic. You have to face that fact, Ruth. Black magic and doing evil things are against everything I believe in. They are against my moral framework. Joining your coven is simply not going to happen."

"You're so lame. It's obvious I didn't raise you."

I laughed. "Yes, it is, thank goodness."

"I sense ambiguity in you, though."

"What do you mean?"

"You've grown in power as a witch, right? I can tell. You

enjoy having more power because it makes your magic more effective. You can do more things with it. That's kinda cool. And the power is a boost to your ego, too, right? It's okay to admit it."

"Sure. I bet every witch feels that way."

"I did, too," she said. "Until I reached a limit, a glass ceiling. There's a lot you can't do with white magic. And a lot of spells only go so far. Black magic opened my eyes. It's like a doorway to a whole new world."

"A dark, corrupt world. I use magic to heal and to help people. Not to hurt them."

"Black magic isn't just about hurting people. You can simply manipulate them to do things they normally wouldn't. You can change their minds on things."

"Manipulating is harmful in its own way," I replied.

She blew cigarette smoke in my face. "You're lying to me and to yourself."

I shook my head.

"Yeah, you are. Like I said, you act like your morals are squeaky clean. But there's a part of you that wants to see what you could do with black magic. To find out how much more you could achieve."

"No."

She cackled. "Deny it all you want, but know it's true. My powers let me see into souls and look for opportunities. Your soul—it ain't as pristine as you think, daughter."

"Can I leave now?"

"Yeah. And you're welcome to come back if you change your mind. I'll warn you, though. Get in my way, and I'll kill you."

"You failed when you tried to do that before."

"I won't fail this time. I'm much more powerful now."

I left the kitchen and ran smack into Lord Arseton. Instead of reacting with anger and his typical haughtiness, he apologized.

"You will learn soon that your mother is truly a saint," he added.

"I better not learn that you harmed any animals at the sanctuary. If you do, I'm coming after you."

"The Knights Simplar have no interest in harming animals. Our mission is to rid the world of foul creatures from hell. Like shifters. Witches like you used to be on our list of enemies until we followed your mother. She showed us that magic is consistent with our mission, and the angel, Myron, agrees."

I shook my head as I walked past him. He jumped in front of me to block my way.

"She's free to go, Arseton," Ruth said from the kitchen doorway.

He nodded at me, and I left the apartment. It was tempting to write off the Knights Simplar as losers with a confused ideology, but their confusion and muddled thinking was what made them dangerous.

I had the worst luck in the world. Not only was my mother back in my life, creating evil. But now, she had these losers following her orders.

I stepped outside and noted the apartment building's location. So much for blindfolding me on the way here, losers.

As if to mock me, Myron, the floating-eyeball cacodemon, hung in the air above me until my ride share arrived to pick me up.

Early the next morning, my doorbell rang. My doorbell camera revealed no one standing at the door, but I opened it anyway. Some package-delivery companies ring the bell when they leave a box on your doormat.

There was no box, but an envelope. And it wasn't on my doormat. It floated in the air at eye level. While I stared at it dumbfounded, it wiggled as if to encourage me to take it.

Finally, I did. The envelope was heavyweight, high-quality cream-colored paper sealed with wax. I opened it and withdrew an invitation on thick, cream card stock. The fancy calligraphy said:

You are invited to join Jellyfish Beach's only coven of witches, led by the all-powerful sorceress, Saint Ruth. Henceforth, no witches will be allowed to practice their craft unless under the supervision of Saint Ruth.

Wow, this was Mafia-like. I had to join the coven or else?

Additional text in red ink magically appeared on the bottom of the invitation:

Failure to comply will result in death.

Oh, so that's the "or else."

It felt wrong to bring the invitation inside my house, but I knew throwing it away would do me no good. I tossed it on the coffee table in the living room, where I rarely sit. I needed time to think about what to do.

CHAPTER 9

UNREAL ESTATE

"I looked up these listings." I waved a stack of computer printouts at Matt before he even stepped through my front door.

"It makes me nervous that you took those from Mr. Bokor's house," he said.

"The police had every opportunity to take them if they'd wanted. They didn't. I thought you believed in aggressive journalism."

"I do. But I don't believe in getting myself arrested."

"Anyway, most of these are still on the market. Mr. Bokor was obviously interested in them, though. And six of them were recently purchased by an entity called Loa Development. I looked it up the way you taught me and found it registered under the name of Jules Bobideau. AKA Mr. Bokor."

"Six?"

"Yeah, purchased for just under three million bucks for the lot of them."

Matt whistled. "Wow. He had lots of cash on hand."

"If they were selling pets to rich people, I'm sure it was a cash business. And they could earn a lot. I'm wondering if Mr. Bokor was getting cash from other sources as well. Like laundering cash for Igor."

"You mean from his scam factory? It looks like that income has dried up."

"Yeah, from scams. Igor could have been lying about freeing all his mesmerized slaves, though. Or maybe he did that after all this cash was earned. And Igor could be up to schemes we're not aware of."

"Igor's my best bet as the source of much of the cash Mr. Bokor had," Matt said. "The question is, would his dealings with Igor cause Igor to kill him?"

"That's what we need to find out. Let's ask around."

When Matt and I arrived at the Jellyfish Beach Executive Suites, Eva at the front desk greeted us with a smile. It immediately turned into a frown when Matt asked if she knew about Mr. Bokor's real estate dealings.

"You'd have to ask Brad. He might know about them." She pointed to the office with a Sunburst Realty nameplate just down the hall.

"Is he in there with a client?" Matt asked.

"No. He rarely brings clients here."

"Why?"

"He says it's because of Jules' incense and the strange

noises that came from his office, but I think he believes renting an office here makes him look small-time. Most of his competitors are affiliated with larger realty agencies."

"But this is such a nice place." He put on his most charming smile for the pretty Latina. "And such nice support staff."

"Were you flirting with her?" I asked as we headed down the hall.

"I'm a reporter. I need to foster sources wherever I go."

"Yeah, right."

I knocked on the door of Brad Keeble of Sunburst Realty.

"Just a minute," came a voice from within.

The door opened. Brad's comb-over was mussed up. He looked like we'd awakened him from a nap.

"Oh. It's you guys again. I was hoping it was a new client."

"Do clients just show up here like that?" Matt asked.

"Actually, no. What do you need to know? You haven't found out who killed Jules?"

"Not yet," I said. "We're here to talk about real estate."

Brad's brown eyes brightened. "Come on in. Are you guys a married couple? There are some great new listings on the market."

"Alas, no," Matt said, pulling his narrow reporter's notebook from his back pants pocket. "We wanted to ask you about Mr. Bokor's involvement in the real estate market."

"In what way?" He didn't seem confused; he seemed evasive.

"Flipping homes."

"Ah. Yes. Jules had a side hustle."

"Side hustle? Spending millions on homes seems a bit grander than that."

"Yes. I meant being a voodoo sorcerer was his passion—and he'd established a reasonable business. But in his greed, he turned to real estate for the big money."

"And where did he get the cash to buy these homes to flip?" Matt asked.

"I don't get into clients' personal affairs."

"Ah, so he was a client!" Matt said with a big, fake smile. "You handled his real estate transactions?"

"Well, yes. I mean, I'm just down the hall from his office, after all. I have a good read on this market. Prices have been so crazy, and the inventory is low. You can't make money as a flipper in a market like this without an expert like me. I also brought in a lot of contractors who remodeled the homes Jules bought before he sold them at a profit."

"Why aren't you working for a larger agency?" I asked.

"I used to." He shook his head as if from bad memories. "But why give a cut to them when I can do just as well on my own? I'm. . . what's the term? A maverick." A strand of his comb-over fell over his eye.

"Yes, of course," I replied.

"Were you involved in Jules' side hustle as more than his agent?" Matt asked. "Like, were you an investor, too?"

"I don't see why that's any of your bus—"

"The man was murdered."

"Um, yes. Poor guy. Look, I made a little money from the commissions, and I used it to go in with Jules on some projects."

"A *little* money?"

"I charged higher than the usual rate because of the extra value I brought to the table."

Matt's look was skeptical.

"I brought my unique expertise," Brad added.

"And your silence," I said.

"What do you mean?"

"Covering up Jules' source of his cash. For instance, if he was laundering money coming from illegal sources."

"Look, I've told the police everything they wanted to know."

"I wouldn't put too much weight on that," Matt said. "The Jellyfish Beach Police Department is not famous for crime solving. Did you tell them about the special projects you did with Jules?"

"Um, no. They weren't as persistent as you."

"Then, why don't you tell me? You're right that I'm very persistent. In fact, I'll crawl so deep into your business that you'll think you have a tapeworm. I'll find dirty stuff in your past that has nothing whatsoever to do with Jules. Or you can work with me amicably as a journalist's trusted source who is cooperating out of civic responsibility."

It always amused me to see Matt's obnoxiously aggressive side.

Brad turned pale. And he was already pasty white for a non-vampire. He gulped for air.

"I don't have to tell you this, and it's nothing worth reporting about," he said, gulping again. "But out on Dead Armadillo Road, just outside of town, there's a lot of undeveloped land."

I knew it well. Many werewolf patients of mine had hunted in those woods and meadows when they shifted. But that was before the land drew the attention of developers.

"Anyway, a big parcel went on the market, zoned commercial and retail," Brad continued. "Jules wanted to buy it and build a shopping center and offices. Even with all his money, he needed more to pull this off. He looked for investors. And I signed on."

Matt and I nodded to encourage him to go on.

"I put a lot of money into this venture. More than I should have. I won't give a dollar amount, but let's just say I put my retirement at risk. But a few weeks ago, Jules backed out. His source of cash had suddenly dried up."

"Did you get your investment back?" Matt asked.

Brad shook his head. "Only a little. Jules had already blown through it, along with his own cash."

"On what?"

"Danged if I know."

"That must have made you very angry at him," Matt said.

"Look, if you're implying it gave me a motive to kill him, you're dead wrong. Oops, bad wording. You're egregiously mistaken. Jules said he was working on getting my money back for me. With him dead, that's now impossible."

"I'm sorry to hear that," I said.

"No one's as sorry as I am."

Actually, Jules was the sorriest one of all.

"Thank you for your candor, Mr. Keeble," Matt said, rising from his chair. "We're sorry for all you've been through."

"Sorry for your loss," I said. "I mean, the loss of your partner. Well, the loss of your money, too, but it seems gauche to put it that way."

Matt rescued me. "I might contact you again with additional questions."

Eva, the receptionist, watched us with interest as we came down the hall toward her desk. She must know a lot of secrets about the tenants here.

"Brad seemed furious at Jules. Would you agree?" I asked her.

She nodded enthusiastically. "They had a big fight just before Jules was murdered."

"Oh, really? About what?"

"Money. I don't know the details."

"Did you mention that to the police?"

"I shouldn't divulge things I overhear in these offices, but the detective asked if I knew of anyone angry at Jules. I had to tell her."

"Of course." I thanked her on our way out.

"Oh, my. That was quite an interview," I said to Matt as we pulled out of the parking lot beside the space reserved for 1-800-MR-BOKOR.

"Yeah. He sounds guilty to me."

"And aren't you the hard-nosed reporter?"

"I don't get many opportunities to interview a murder suspect. Here in Jellyfish Beach, my big journalistic scoops tend to be about pooper-scooper laws."

"Should we share our thoughts with Detective Shortle?"

"Nah, not yet," he replied, flipping through the pages of his notebook. "I think we need to investigate the other side of Mr. Bokor's 'side hustles.' Namely, Igor, the principal supplier of cash to Mr. Bokor—I mean Jules. No, Jules sounds funny when referring to that guy."

"I've met him, and you're correct. Jules sounds much too sophisticated for him. Not to speak ill of the dead."

"Let's speak about the undead instead. Igor could have many motives for killing Mr. Bokor. He wants us to believe it would be insane to kill the producer of the lucrative chimera pets and Igor's future scammers. But what if Mr. Bokor didn't want to make chimeras anymore? Maybe it's stressful and tiring."

"Puts a toll on your soul."

"Exactly. Or maybe he *was* laundering the extra cash that came from other sources, and he wasn't supposed to spend it, just hold it for Igor. Or put it somewhere other than real estate."

"Yes, and Igor wanted to stop the big real estate development that Mr. Bokor and Brad were up to," I speculated.

"Could be. Can you get us an appointment with Igor? I have to admit that interrogating a vampire is a lot more difficult than a human, and not just because he could tear your head off at any moment."

"I'll text him. But not now. Don't want to wake him."

"Right. We don't want a cranky vampire."

As soon as the sun went down, I sent my text. To my relief, Igor answered right away and said we could come to his house that same evening.

Maybe Matt was right that Igor was attracted to me.

We took Matt's truck because it was less likely to get stuck in Igor's long, sandy driveway. As usual, Matt complained about the setting.

"Look, another skeleton is hanging from that tree! What's the deal with this? It freaks me out. Should we report the skeletons to the police? Have there been many disappearances of food-delivery drivers?"

"We're not sure those are actual human remains," I replied, "and not an art installation."

"Yeah. I guess I would have heard through my sources if many people have gone missing. Still, who would consider hanging skeletons to be art?"

"A vampire who's so rich he doesn't care what art critics think."

Igor answered the door with his usual enthusiasm, his cheeks flushed as if he had just fed. There was a pizza box lying outside the door. He ignored it. Because he hadn't ordered pizza for dinner; he'd ordered a pizza-delivery person.

"Have you learned anything about who killed Mr. Bokor?" he asked. "Or found any of our escaped human hybrids?"

"We found the elephant-human hybrid," I replied. "He had come to Mr. Bokor's house looking for something."

"Just so you know, he was *not* how I wanted the elephant hybrids to turn out. I wanted them to be more human."

"Yeah, this poor guy probably wouldn't succeed as a scammer."

"What happened to him? Did the Cryptids Society whisk him away?"

"Yes. They're interviewing and examining him as we speak."

"If he's still alive," Igor said.

"Of course, he's still alive. I totally disagree with your theory that the Society would kill anyone."

"Then what are they going to do with the hybrid? They can't simply release him into human society."

"They have a sanctuary for cryptids where he can live happily and safely."

"Do you honestly believe that?"

I hesitated. Did I?

"Yes, I do."

"Evidently, you have more faith in them than I do," Igor said with a sneer.

"I've been working with them now for several months, and I've seen nothing but professionalism and a passion for cryptids and all supernatural creatures. The folks in the Society are a bit weird, but anyone would be in that line of work. Like me."

"Totally," Matt added.

I gave him the stink eye.

"I don't believe they killed Mr. Bokor," I said.

Igor's cat-dog jumped into my lap. Her tail wagged, which concerned me. The tail was on the dog body, so you'd expect to see it wagging when greeting a visitor. But the creature had a cat's head. Did that mean she had a cat brain? If so, the wagging tail meant she was agitated and ready to attack.

"Don't mind Nelly," Igor said. "I think she likes you."

"Does she have the brain of a cat or dog?"

"Her brain appears to be a hybrid. She's loyal and eager to please like a dog, but she also knows how to use a litter box. She's the best of both worlds. Mr. Bokor's magic is miraculous."

"Congratulations. At least one of his chimeras turned out well."

"On the whole, the pets he created were a success. And quite lucrative."

"That brings us to why we're here," Matt said. "Mr. Bokor had a lot of money to burn. Something you don't see in voodoo sorcerers."

"You haven't seen any other voodoo sorcerers," I told Matt.

"True. But I haven't seen them on the lists of top-paying professions."

"Yes," Igor said. "I helped make Mr. Bokor fantastically wealthy."

"From selling the hybrid pets?" Matt asked.

"Correct. He supplied the magic, and I connected him with super-wealthy clients. I also paid him for his work developing the human-animal hybrids."

"Did you have any disgruntled clients?"

"None. All love the pets that we sold them."

"Were you aware Mr. Bokor invested heavily in real estate by flipping houses?" I asked.

"Of course. He could do whatever he wanted with his money."

"Are you aware of a giant development project he was planning and then backed out of?"

Igor nodded. "I might have invested a bit in that venture."

"Might have? You mean you're uncertain?"

"In case you haven't noticed, I have quite a bit of money. Sometimes, I'm lax in keeping track of where I spend it."

"Mr. Stanisloopsky, do you know of anyone whom Mr.

Bokor cheated or angered through his real estate dealings, or even his pet sales?" Matt asked.

"No, I don't. That's why I believe the Friends of Cryptids Society was behind his death."

It was time to move this conversation in a new direction. I wanted to find out if Mr. Bokor was laundering money for Igor, but I couldn't think of a diplomatic way to ask if they were up to illegal activity.

"I don't mean to be rude," I said, "but may I ask you how *you* became so rich and successful?"

"You're not rude at all. My father was a noble in Poland during the Middle Ages. I inherited his land and title. After I was turned and a few centuries passed, I grew bored with being the landed gentry. I sold most of my land and estates and went into banking. Eventually, I made my way to America, where I financed many of the robber barons when they were first starting out. I grew bored with that, too, and moved to Florida, first to Palm Beach, and then to Jellyfish Beach."

"Why on earth would you move from Palm Beach to this place?" Matt asked.

"I feared word was spreading that I was a vampire. I needed to get away from the idle rich with all their gossip and go somewhere underpopulated. When I arrived, there were only farmers and fishermen here. No one knew anything about me."

"What streams of revenue do you have now, besides selling hybrid pets?" I asked. "Was your telemarketing company created only to punish the scammers you enslaved, or was it actually profitable?"

"It began as a way to torture the lowlifes who went into business to scam people. I used them to raise money for legitimate charities. Then, I realized how much money I could make running a scam factory myself. Not that I needed the money. It's just so much fun earning it."

"Isn't that hypocritical?" Matt asked.

I cringed. Why was he provoking a vampire?

Igor laughed. "When you've lived through century after century, boredom is your greatest enemy. And ethics seem silly and irrelevant. Hypocrisy is meaningless to me. After all, I'm a monster. Literally."

"Were your profits from the scam factory attracting scrutiny from law enforcement?"

"Yes. That's why I laundered my money through Mr. Bokor!"

Oh, my. He just went and admitted to what I was afraid to ask him.

"The concept of money laundering is that it ends up back in your pocket after it's been cleaned," Matt said. "Did it make its way back to you?"

"Much of it did not."

"Is it held up because Mr. Bokor died, or did he do something with it?"

"Both. It sounds like you are asking if I had a motive for killing him."

"Absolutely not," I lied.

He chuckled. "Yes, you are. If you recall, when my financial advisor was staked after he defrauded me—and many others—you suspected I killed him. You soon found out that I did not. I obviously don't care if I lose a million here, a few million there. I'm sorry to disappoint you if that's why you came here tonight."

"We're just looking for clues to solve his murder," I said. "You don't care if you lose millions, but a lot of other people would."

"I hope you find them. And don't ignore other motives. You need to take seriously my theory that the Friends of Cryptids Society killed him. And don't forget the other obvious motive."

Matt and I stared at him stupidly.

"The anger a monster feels toward his creator."

Igor was right. A human chimera was still on the loose—the centaur named Trevor. He was still a primary suspect for the murder of Mr. Bokor.

And if Trevor killed him, he could kill others.

We thanked Igor and headed out into the night. Despite knowing there were vampires, werewolves, and other supernatural creatures in Jellyfish Beach, I'd always felt safe living here. I understood monsters. They were more predictable than demented human criminals—of which our town thankfully had very few.

The escaped hybrid was a monster with the added danger of being part human. And he was out there, somewhere, right now.

I now fully understood why the Society so desperately wanted to bring him in.

CHAPTER 10

A BEEF WITH THE BOKOR

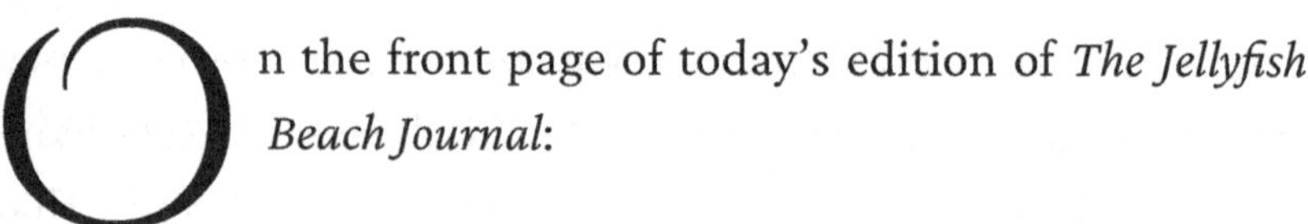

On the front page of today's edition of *The Jellyfish Beach Journal*:

POLICE: NO SUSPECTS IN VOODOO MURDER

Matthew Rosen, Senior Staff Writer

JELLYFISH BEACH – In the week since a professed voodoo sorcerer was stabbed to death in a Jellyfish Beach parking lot, local police have yet to identify a suspect. Becka Tribeca, spokesperson for the department, said detectives are interviewing "more than one" person of interest.

On October 10th, Jules Bobideau was found dead in a dumpster behind the parking lot shared by the Good-to-Go convenience store and the Jellyfish Beach Mystical Mart & Botanica on Sixth Street. Police say the victim, who owns the business 1-800-MR-BOKOR, was killed in his nearby car before being placed in the dumpster in an attempt to hide the body. A witness who found the body said the victim had shopped in the botanica prior to the attack.

Forensic evidence indicates the victim died of both incision and puncture wounds, police said. The weapon was a cylindrical tool, possibly an ice pick or screwdriver.

Mr. Bobideau, originally from Haiti, had lived in Jellyfish Beach for 45 years. The Journal has been unable to reach any family members for statements.

The receptionist at the Jellyfish Beach Executive Suites where the victim rented an office, Eva Martin, said, "Jules was the best—and only—voodoo sorcerer I have ever known. He will be missed."

Anyone with information should call the Jellyfish Beach Police Tip Hotline at 561-I-SNITCH.

I READ Matt's article as I sat at the botanica's front counter shortly after opening the shop. Why did it bother me that Matt had contacted Eva for a quote? The insistent ticking of the grandfather clock filled the store, empty of customers, like it was poking me, insisting that I find the answer.

I didn't have time to. The bells above the door tinkled, and Madame Tibodet came in, followed by Carl the Zombie.

"Good morning, my love," she said in her musical Caribbean accent. "I'm looking for some mandrake root."

"It's in a cabinet on the rear wall. I'll get it for you."

"No, no. You stay seated. I will get it."

While she moved her stocky figure down the center aisle, Carl remained near me, stroking the ceramic black cat that sat on the counter. He loved that figurine. I was tempted to give it to him as a gift, but it belonged to Luisa, and I wanted to check with her to see if it was okay.

"It's funny," I said to Madame Tibodet. "Mr. Bokor bought some mandrake on the night he was murdered. I hope you're not using it for sorcery like he was."

"Banish the thought!" she said angrily as she returned to the counter with the plastic baggie. "I would never do any of the things that wicked man did. I'm a priestess who wants nothing to do with sorcery."

"You know the local voodoo community well. Did he have any angry clients?"

"He had too many to count. He was a dishonorable man. I'll never forgive him for what he did to Carl and me."

I don't know how or why Mr. Bokor chose Carl to turn into a zombie, but he went so far as to steal Carl's recently dead body from the morgue before performing the magical ritual that reanimated the corpse. He must have done it simply for the large sum of money he charged Madame Tibodet and would have received from someone else if she had refused.

She had been mortified by her brother's transformation, but she couldn't allow him to be sold to some stranger. To her, it felt like paying ransom for a hostage.

I could never figure out if Madame Tibodet took a small

amount of comfort in having her brother still in her life, or if it was a nightmare for her. Carl reminded her every day that her brother was dead, despite his undead body shambling along behind her, a mere shadow of his former self.

A sharp *crack* came from my left. I turned to find Carl had snapped off the head of the ceramic cat.

"I am so sorry," Madame Tibodet said, I guess to both of us. "I should never have uttered that man's evil name out loud. Of course, I will pay for the figurine."

"Don't worry about it." I hoped Luisa wouldn't be mad.

The bells announced another customer. Madame Tibodet ushered Carl into a nearby closet to prevent freaking out the person.

It turned out to not be a customer. It was Detective Shortle.

"Good morning, Detective," I said. "Any updates?"

"Actually, Mrs. Tibodet here is whom I was looking for. Ma'am, you haven't returned my calls. I went to your home this morning, and a neighbor told me you might be here."

"What do you want from me?"

"I just want to ask you a few questions. Nothing to be concerned about."

"The police don't come around looking to make friends. What am I accused of?"

"Nothing, ma'am."

"What am I suspected of? Tell me why you want to talk to me."

"It's about Jules Bobideau, Mr. Bokor. I've interviewed a number of his clients, and one said you had a beef with Mr. Bokor."

A moan came from the closet. I cleared my throat loudly in a clumsy attempt to cover it up.

Shortle looked at me and the closet, confusion on her face.

"This client wants to tarnish my name, and you just haul me into jail? That's how it works in my old country."

"Not at all, ma'am. I just want to ask you a few questions, then you can go home. Please come with me."

"Ask me your questions here."

"Ma'am, I'm asking you politely to come with me. You're not obligated to do so. But I warn you, I might get a warrant for your arrest if you don't come voluntarily."

Carl moaned again in the closet.

"What is that noise?" Shortle asked.

"A hot-water pipe that needs fixing," I said.

I immediately cast a spell to seal the closet door. Carl lurching out to defend his sister would not go over well.

"Okay, I'll do as you ask," Madame Tibodet said. "Do I need a lawyer?"

"No. But we can't stop you from having one."

"I'll call Paul Leclerc," I told Madame Tibodet. I don't think she knew him, but he was my go-to attorney for protecting supernaturals and those associated with them. He was a werewolf, after all.

Shortle glared at me as she walked toward the door, followed by Madame Tibodet.

"Don't get in my way," Shortle said to me. "Or I'll bring you in next."

What a shame. I know she must be under great pressure to make progress on this case. But until now, I had thought we had built the beginning of a beautiful friendship.

"We've already broken into his house," Matt complained when I called him. "Now you want to break into his office, too?"

"Yes, of course," I replied. "How can we solve his murder if we don't search Mr. Bokor's office? There could be valuable information about that big real estate deal. We need to find out why it fell through, and what Mr. Bokor did with all the money from Brad, Igor, and the other investors."

"I'm sure the police have already searched there. And look what they did—brought in Madame Tibodet for questioning."

"Shortle doesn't seem to know or care about the big real estate deal. And I'm worried about Madame Tibodet. I can't believe she would kill the man, but she didn't hide how much she hated him. We need to find a more likely suspect and take the heat off her."

Matt relented, and I immediately drove to his bungalow to pick him up. When we arrived at the office building where the executive suites were located, the parking lot was empty. After all, it was 10:30 p.m., and even the cleaning crews had left.

The door to the lobby was locked, but my unlocking spell took care of that quickly. The elevator required a key card to go anywhere, so we took the stairs to the second floor. Entering the floor also required a key card. One spell later, we were standing in front of the glass doors of the Jellyfish Beach Executive Suites with the front desk just beyond.

Yet another unlocking spell was necessary. Before we went inside, I had to disarm the security system, the keypad for which was visible on the wall to the right of the door.

I'll admit that I had little experience with turning off alarms. Why would I? I'm not a burglar-witch. But I knew the challenge was that I couldn't simply fry the circuits, because the alarm-monitoring company would be alerted of the disruption. This had to be done properly.

Clutching my power charm in my left hand, I recited the incantation and felt the energy flow from me into the alarm-control keypad. There, it detected the psychic energy of the many fingers of tenants who had disarmed the system when they were the first to arrive in the morning and had armed it when they were the last to leave.

Four numerical keys, plus the arm and disarm keys, had been pressed twice a day, every day. The images of these keys came into my mind in the proper sequence.

"Okay, let's go," I said, stepping through the unlocked door and heading straight for the keypad while the alarm made its warning beeps. Holding my breath, I entered the code from the mental image and then the disarm button.

The warning beeps stopped.

"Thank goodness," I said.

"You weren't sure it would work?"

"It's only the second time I've used this spell."

"Well, save your energy," Matt said. "You have another door to unlock."

But when we arrived at Mr. Bokor's office, Matt tried the door and found it unlocked.

"Hmm, that's a bit odd," he said.

He turned on the overhead light, and the office looked like I remembered it from when I had come here with Madame Tibodet. No possessions had been packed into boxes or removed. I guessed the executive suites' management was waiting for Mr. Bokor's next-of-kin, whoever they were, to handle it.

On the red plush rug in the center of the office were signs a family member of sorts had been here: hoof impressions.

"Looks like our friend Trevor has been here. I wonder why."

"Feeding the snake, for starters."

The ball python in the glass terrarium had a large bulge in its belly.

"But was he also searching for something?"

It would be difficult to tell. One wall of the office resembled a botanica, with shelves covered in bottles of potions and baggies of powders and herbs. A small bookcase nearby held spell books and published books about voodoo, hoodoo, and magic in general.

A single two-drawer file cabinet sat beside the desk. The lock took only seconds for my spell to unlock. The drawers were stuffed with manila folders that held invoices for sorcery services rendered, many of which were cures for ailments and curses against enemies.

I saw nothing related to real estate. It looked like Mr. Bokor kept his revenue streams completely separated.

Matt sat behind the desk and opened the two side drawers. The left one contained a small drum and several rattles. The other held only a bottle of rum.

The shallow center drawer had a few pens, several paper-clips, and a floor plan of the executive suites.

"Why does he need that?" I asked, looking over Matt's shoulder. "Everyone here has their name on their door."

The square that corresponded with this office had been

circled with a yellow highlighter. Numbers were written in pencil inside two office squares and in the reception area by the front desk. One of the numbers had been erased. They meant nothing to me.

"He must have gotten this plan when he first leased his office," Matt said.

I noticed a closed door in the corner.

"We forgot to check the closet."

It was locked, of course. I cast the unlocking spell and got an unpleasant surprise.

The door was sealed with magic. Unfamiliar magic.

I placed my hands on the cracks on either side of the door and used a probing spell to identify the magic I was up against.

It wasn't elemental magic; a bitter taste filled my mouth that indicated Mr. Bokor had used black magic of some sort. Just like anyone would be, I was now more determined to get the door open.

I explained to Matt that I needed to figure out how to defeat the seal.

"There's got to be something really good in there," he said, feeling the same way I did.

All I could identify was an African origin of the magic; it was most likely rooted in the Yoruba religion as so many New World religions, such as voodoo, hoodoo, obeah, and Santeria, were. But it wasn't like any of the spells I'd encountered from the magic systems of those religions. The spell must have been of Mr. Bokor's own creation.

Normally, I can picture how a spell is constructed—the way strands of energy are woven together to construct the framework. I can often see even the "extras" that are added to it through powders, potions, and the incantations.

Tonight, though, I was stumped by this magic that sealed the door. My probing spell was still active, though, and if I directed it elsewhere, it might pick up clues to the inner workings of the magic Mr. Bokor was using.

I stepped back from the closet door, glancing around the office to find something else to probe.

"What are you doing?" Matt asked.

I ignored him, maintaining my concentration and my probing spell. Then, I remembered what was in the desk drawer.

The small drum. It must have a ritualistic purpose.

I moved to the desk and sat in its chair. When I opened the left drawer, I moved the focus of my spell from the closet door to the drum. The drum was brimming with energy.

Soon, a vision of his magic formed in my mind. It was like a blueprint of how the spell was constructed. I speak about magic with words like "energy," but a spell is not a mere blast of power. My spells are woven together, and energy serves as the threads.

However, unlike my spells, this black magic was structured like flesh. It resembled muscle fibers and blood vessels, with ligaments and cartilage. This flesh was not healthy but decomposing.

I sat silently for a while, absorbing this information. Matt was wise enough to keep his mouth shut.

Then I returned to the closet door, putting my hands on the cracks again.

And I saw it: the basic structure of the magic sealing the door. I now used my negation spell to deconstruct and cancel Mr. Bokor's enchantment, its magical fibers and ligaments falling apart.

I tried the door again, and it opened.

"Woah!" Matt said.

The closet was larger than I had expected. And it was empty, aside from a gurney, a small table, and floor-stand candelabra.

The closet smelled of decomposition.

"Was this where he made his zombies?" Matt asked from right behind me, startling me.

"I think so."

"How messed up is that? He brought dead bodies to an office building? Why didn't he do this in some deserted self-storage facility?"

I didn't answer. I broke my probing spell and reached out to an item that had caught my eye.

A thick notebook lay on the small table. It was the kind of spiral-bound notebook students use.

I opened it and flipped through pages filled with dense handwriting in black ink. Fortunately, it was in English, so I could decipher it despite the tight cursive lettering.

The pages held the instructions for creating chimeras using a combination of alchemy, voodoo, and the unknown magic that had sealed the door.

"I'm ready to go now," I said. "Let's get out of this creepy place."

The search of Mr. Bokor's office had been a bust until now. I would give the notebook to Mrs. Lupis and Mr. Lopez, who would hopefully forgive me for failing to photograph the centaur.

For some reason, getting back in their good graces felt extremely important to me.

CHAPTER 11
WEREWOLF DID HE GO?

My phone rang the following afternoon, right after I returned home from the botanica. I was hoping it would be Paul Leclerc or Madame Tibodet with news of her exoneration. Instead, my phone said the caller was Cynthia Roarke. I assumed the werewolf wanted to make a home-health appointment for her and her husband.

"Missy, Harry is missing!"

"Oh, my. For how long?"

"He left two nights ago. He said he was in the mood for hunting. That was the last I heard from him. You remember the last time he went missing after shifting?"

"Sure do." He once had a blackout-like incident after turning from wolf back to human form. He had to make his way home from the mall with no clothes on.

"I've contacted the police, but they've done nothing. And there are no signs of foul play. Can you use your magic to find him?"

"Yes, of course. I'll try my locator spell. Gather his most beloved possession, and I'll be there shortly."

When I arrived at the Roarkes' condo in Seaweed Manor, Cynthia handed me a rawhide bone from a pet store.

"What's this?" I asked.

"His favorite chew toy."

"Are you serious?"

"As you know, the full moon makes us shift involuntarily. It's not like recreational shifting. And if the moon comes at an inconvenient time, or when you don't feel like going out, chewing on these takes away some of the urge to kill. It's kind of relaxing, you know."

"Okay." I gingerly took the heavily gnawed-upon dried cow skin from her. Thank goodness it wasn't wet and slimy with wolf spit.

In Cynthia's kitchen, I drew a magic circle with a dry-erase marker and sat in the center, surrounded by five lighted candles. The candles were at the points of a pentagram, each representing one of the five elements: earth, air, water, fire, and spirit.

Unlike in my mother's black-magic circle, this pentagram was right side up.

I held the rawhide in both hands while I kneeled and recited the invocation, my inner energies converging and warming my body from the inside out. I extracted Harry's psychic energy from the rawhide, and there was plenty of it to work with. He had put a lot of passion into chewing on this bone.

Soon, a glowing orb appeared, floating in the air above the rawhide.

I whispered, "Spirit of Harry Roarke, go find the soul to which you belong."

The orb floated across the kitchen, increased its speed, and passed through a nearby window. At the same time, I went into a trance-like state. Soon, a vision appeared as if I looked at the world from the orb's perspective.

The orb raced west across Jellyfish Beach toward the last light of the setting sun. Leaving the city limits, it passed above sprawling housing developments that gave way to farmland where fruits and vegetables grew. It flew above a forested area and a river that sliced through it.

Finally, the orb stopped above a large parcel of cleared land, then descended.

The property was a compound of buildings, and large enclosed pens. I soon recognized it: the Morris Wildlife Refuge. The facility rescued and rehabilitated injured wild animals and relocated healthy ones that had lost their habitat because of development.

This was the organization that had its gala ruined by my mother.

The orb zeroed in on a pen enclosed by a wire-mesh fence. It had feeding and watering troughs as well as various covered shelters. Pacing back and forth was a large wolf with gray hair streaked with white.

It was Harry in wolf form.

Why was he here? Why hadn't he shifted back to human form? His hind leg was bandaged. Perhaps that explained why.

I broke my spell and, once I regained my bearings, reported my findings to Cynthia.

"We love that place," she said. "Especially the panthers and bear cubs. But I don't know why Harry would go there in wolf form. Even if he was injured, our werewolf healing abilities should have been sufficient. And, yes, it makes no sense that he didn't shift back to human. Let's go there when they open in the morning and ask for Harry back."

"It might not be that easy. There aren't any wolves in the wild in Florida anymore. We'd have to say he's a pet, but we'd need to show them a permit for owning restricted animals. It might be easier to sneak in, cut the fence, and do a jailbreak."

"No, Missy, it's too risky. I'm sure they have security cameras everywhere. Harry and I are retired, but you're still working. You can't afford to get arrested."

She was right. I thought of myself as law-abiding, so why did I suggest such a thing?

"Let's go there tomorrow," I said. "We'll say hi to Harry and see how he responds. We need to find out why he hasn't shifted back to human."

"And didn't bother to let me know where he was and that he was safe."

"THAT IS NOT what I wanted to see," I said when Cynthia and I arrived at the sanctuary the next morning in her mammoth SUV.

A police car was parked at the gate.

"Yeah, they're not here to break up a raucous raccoon party."

We bypassed the visitors' entrance and headed straight for the pen where I had seen Harry.

The wire-mesh on one side of the enclosure had a gaping hole. Harry was gone.

I approached a group of volunteers in their sanctuary T-shirts who watched a police officer speak with an employee.

"Did the wolf escape?" I asked.

"Yes. Vandals cut the enclosure," said a female volunteer.

"I think they stole the wolf," her older colleague said.

"He was a very rare wolf," a third woman told me. "Extremely large and didn't have a tail."

I wasn't going to tell her he was a werewolf.

"How did you acquire him in the first place?" I asked. "There are no wolves in the wild around here."

"He simply showed up. We found him two mornings ago lying outside the clinic, severely injured with a shard of glass in his leg. We patched him up right away and were going to keep him here until we could find out if he escaped from a zoo or migrated to South Florida."

I returned to Cynthia and repeated what the volunteers had told me.

"That makes no sense," Cynthia said. "Harry's leg would have healed instantly from a wound like that."

It made me wonder if it really had been a shard of glass that injured him. I asked the volunteers where I could find the medical director. They pointed to a thin man in khaki shorts among the group speaking with the police officer.

"Excuse me, Doctor," I whispered to him. "May I ask you a question?"

He nodded.

"The missing wolf—was it a shard of glass that injured him?"

"No, it was the strangest thing. A throwing star. You know, those weapons with the pointed blades like the ninjas use?"

"Yes."

"And it appeared to be made of silver. It was lodged in the wolf's leg, and he was nearly at the point of death. That struck me as odd because he hadn't lost much blood and wasn't infected. After I removed the star, cleaned the wound, and sutured it, he recovered surprisingly quickly."

"Any idea who would have taken him?"

"I'm assuming it's whoever attacked him with the star. That's not a weapon a hunter or hiker would have."

I thanked him and ushered Cynthia from the property.

"He was attacked with a silver weapon," I said. "Obviously, it was someone who knew he's a werewolf. Let's go to your condo so I can cast another locator spell. We need to rescue him right away."

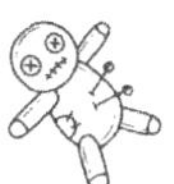

HARRY'S beloved rawhide chew toy had lost most of his psychic energy when my spell had converted it into the orb, which then returned the energy to Harry when the orb found him.

This time, I used an item just as beloved: his motorcycle helmet.

I performed the spell and sent the new orb on its way. It didn't have far to travel. It hovered above a drab apartment complex in town before entering a unit on the second floor and being absorbed by Harry's wolf body as he lay on his side upon the kitchen floor. I didn't need to cross-reference a satellite map to locate the apartment complex because I'd been there before.

It was the home of Tim Tissy, AKA Lord Arseton.

I should have known the Knights Simplar were involved with this. After all, they had known a werewolf was hunting in the forest beside the wildlife sanctuary and must have assumed he lived there, which was why they enlisted Mother to ruin the gala. When he was wounded, he did end up there.

But how had they found Harry in the first place? And who would own a throwing star made of silver? Answer: a freak like Lord Arseton.

The most urgent question of all was whether Harry was okay. I knew he was alive. Otherwise, the orb wouldn't have found him, but I worried about the state of his health. They must have used another silver weapon or tool to subdue him during his capture, which would put him completely at their mercy.

I told Cynthia that I knew where Harry was, but I downplayed the danger.

"Let's go get his butt out of there!" she said. "I'll round up a bunch of bad boys who can bust him out of anywhere."

"But they can't be allowed to shift into wolves. The people who have Harry believe he's a werewolf, but I hope to fool them into thinking they were wrong. I don't want these morons finding any proof that werewolves exist. Are your bad boys bad when they're in human form?"

"They're all retirees, so they're not exactly in their prime. But they're all heavily armed."

"That will have to do. I'll use my magic as extra firepower. For me, magic is mostly meant for healing, but I can immobilize the enemy. I'll need to be in visual contact with them, though, meaning we have to get Arseton to open his door. We can't bring any overly menacing boneheads with us."

"Well, that eliminates most of the residents of Seaweed Manor."

CYNTHIA, formerly a hippie, didn't use guns, but she wanted to come along since it was her husband we were rescuing. Alvin, the stereotypical biker-werewolf type, carried a Glock. Though he was in his sixties, the beefy man looked strong enough to not need his weapon.

The other two "bad boys" were named Bull and Marston. Bull was in his late seventies, and his bull days were long behind him, but he carried more weaponry than a Marine Corps platoon. Marston was the youngest and largest, with a shaved head and a hair-trigger temper. I made it clear that he would *not* be the one who rang the doorbell.

Bull would perform that task, pretending he was a plumber sent here by the landlord because of a broken pipe above Arseton's apartment. His firepower would save us from a sudden, unexpected attack from within until I could cast my sleep spell.

We divided our team and went up two separate flights of stairs, approaching the apartment along the breezeway from opposite directions. Everyone stayed out of view while Bull rang the doorbell and knocked on the door with authority. I held my breath.

No one answered.

Bull knocked several times with too much enthusiasm. He sounded like a SWAT team. I feared a neighbor would come out to see what was going on.

Still no answer.

"No one's there," Bull said, trying the door. It was locked, as expected.

I came up to the door.

"Harry, are you in there? Harry?"

The clicking of claws upon tile came from within.

"Yes. Who is it?" asked a deep, rough voice on the other side of the door.

That's what I believed he said. Most werewolves can make a passable attempt at speech when in wolf form, but it's greatly impaired by the shape of their tongue and muzzle.

For all I know, Harry really said, "Let's poo on it."

I beckoned to Cynthia to come to the door to translate.

"Ask him what happened, and why he's still in wolf form."

She did so, and he whimpered with joy to hear her voice. He answered her with his impeded speech. After he stopped speaking, she translated.

"He said he was ambushed in the woods outside of town. The assailants shot at him, probably with silver bullets, but they missed. Then, he was struck in his leg and found the star imbedded in it. He couldn't remove it because it was silver. He was rapidly losing strength and managed to make it to the wildlife sanctuary before he passed out. When he woke up in the clinic after treatment, they moved him to the outdoor pen."

"Why didn't he shift back to human after he was well again?"

"He said he couldn't, for some reason. Something is wrong with him. He's not sure if it's an infection from the silver. Not being able to shift is the only thing keeping him alive."

"What do you mean?"

"He said he was abducted from the sanctuary by the same guys who had attacked him. They're a bunch of fanatics who want to kill him, but they want him to shift to human first to prove he's not actually a wolf. They're using a silver chain to weaken him and figure he can't stay in this form forever. But he couldn't shift, even if he wanted to, because as soon as he did, they would kill him."

"Wow," I said.

"Can't we break down the door and let him out?"

"I'm casting a spell to unlock the door. Just give me a moment."

The dim yellow lights on the ceiling of the breezeway went out, replaced by a blinding white blaze. I had needed only a minute to create my spell, but time had already run out.

CHAPTER 12
THINGS GET HAIRY

The overhead lights in the breezeway died, yet I was blinded by a small, intense fireball moving toward us just below the ceiling of the open corridor.

"Oh, the witch and her friends have come to visit me," said Lord Arseton's voice. "Whatever could they want with me?"

He was close enough now that I could see him, though he was backlit by the fireball trailing behind him. Below it was a woman. I squinted to discern who she was.

Harriet, the black-magic witch. What was she doing here?

"Well?" Arseton demanded. "Why are you here?"

"I suspect you stole a wolf from the Morris Wildlife Sanctuary. I'm a big supporter of theirs."

"Why would you suspect me?"

"Because you and my mother have been sabotaging the sanctuary."

He smiled like a cartoon villain. "Correct. But what we stole was a werewolf."

"Nonsense."

"I brought Harriet with me because her supernatural senses are sharp enough to verify that he's a werewolf. The way he reacts to silver is a dead giveaway, but he was injured and not up to full strength, so I want to be certain."

Harriet pointed to the floating fireball, and it disappeared, returning the breezeway to its murky yellow light.

"They're all werewolves," Harriet said, gesturing to Cindy and her crew.

"We've hit the jackpot, haven't we?" Arseton said. "And I just happen to have a gun loaded with silver bullets."

He pulled a handgun from the back of his trousers. A silencer was fitted to the muzzle.

As if on cue, our three "bad-boy" soldiers took off, running away from him to the stairwell at the end of the breezeway. I was flabbergasted, having expected them, with all their attitude and weapons, to at least pretend to put up a fight. I guessed silver was an existential horror to them. Cynthia, however, stood her ground.

"Harriet, come inside with me and verify the wolf is a werewolf so I can put him down," Arseton said. "Don't worry, he's too weak to attack you."

"You leave my husband alone!" Cynthia yelled.

"Oh, we have our confirmation already, then. Is it true you're a werewolf, too?"

He aimed his pistol at her as he produced a ring of keys from his pocket.

"You can come inside with us."

The keys dropped to the concrete floor, followed by an unconscious Arseton.

My sleep spell had worked.

The problem was, Harriet was still standing, wide awake.

"I put up a protection spell the moment I saw you," she said with a sneer.

"I didn't know there were black-magic protection spells."

"There are various types of shields. But I used regular magic for this spell, probably one you know. That's the thing self-righteous witches like you never understand. You don't have to choose between darkness and light. You can use black magic along with your regular magic. It's like having extra tools in your toolbox."

She might be right, but what she didn't realize was that black magic corrupts not just your soul but your magical energies. I suspected her protection spell had vulnerabilities.

Harriet knelt and examined Arseton, placing her palms on his cheeks in an intimate way that suggested they might be more than friends. She was, undoubtedly, attempting to break my sleep spell, so I had to work quickly.

I put myself into a semi-trance and opened all my senses, focusing them on Harriet, her aura, and the field of magic that surrounded all witches when they were using magic. I analyzed her spell in the same way I did with Mr. Bokor's magic.

Soon, I saw how Harriet's protection spell was constructed. And, sure enough, I saw flaws in its weave—imperfections caused by the corruption of her magic-making by the evil of black magic.

Remember, black magic uses the power of demons, misery, and death. Of evil. And you must pay a huge price for playing with that. It's like handling radioactive material while building a weapon.

I quickly sent sharp probes of benign energy into my visualization of Harriet's protection spell. They severed weakened strands and separated the loose ones.

Soon, the entire structure fell apart, and the spell was broken.

She looked up at me, startled. Her eyes widened as she realized what I had done.

Then, they closed in repose as she dropped off to sleep.

I grabbed Arseton's key ring, trying three different keys before I found the one that unlocked his door.

"Help me drag them into the apartment before anyone comes by," I told Cynthia.

Together, we moved Arseton and Harriet inside and left them lying on the living-room tile. I turned on the lights and a whimper came from Harry.

The wolf limped toward us as if he carried an enormous weight on his back. What he carried was a sterling silver chain wrapped around his neck.

I tore it off. Cynthia crouched beside him, wrapping him in a big hug.

"Can you shift back to human now?" she asked.

He whimpered and said, "No." Even I could understand that.

"Let's go," I said. "Harry, walk beside Cynthia like a dog on a leash on our way to the SUV, in case anyone sees us."

I tossed the key ring on the floor beside Arseton and turned off the light.

"How long will they stay asleep?" Cynthia asked.

"A few more hours. They'll be fine when they wake up, and you'll be safe at home."

I closed the door behind us, and we went downstairs to the parking lot. Harry walked with more strength now. All his vitality should return now that he was free of any silver. But it troubled me that he couldn't shift. I couldn't think of a reason why.

While we drove to Seaweed Manor, it also troubled me that Harriet had identified the other men as werewolves. Now, the Knights Simplar would be obsessed with looking for them. And destroying them.

I didn't have the time or patience to deal with those buffoons right now. Mr. Bokor's murder needed to be solved, and Trevor was still at large.

Werewolves have existed in our society for centuries without being discovered by the public at large. A visibly half-human, half-horse creature could never pull that off.

And if he was discovered by the public, it would be a calamity.

When Madame Tibodet arrived at the botanica the next day, Luisa and I greeted her warmly and watched her carefully. I desperately wanted her to tell us how the police interview had gone, but I didn't dare ask. I assumed Luisa felt the same.

"How are you, Madame Tibodet?" I inquired. I never called her by her first name, Monique, and she never told me to do so. This severe woman with the tight floral headscarf did not invite familiarity.

In fact, she seemed more severe than ever today.

"I am healthy and grateful to the loas for keeping me so. I have a client meeting me here for a consultation." She glanced at the loudly ticking grandfather clock. "In a few minutes."

Luisa looked like she was about to burst. "That's good."

The two of us stared anxiously at the voodoo priestess.

"I think I will wait for my client in the back room."

"How did it go with the police?" Luisa blurted out.

Madame Tibodet compressed her lips. I didn't think she'd answer.

"It was annoying," she said. "A waste of my time. A police officer had been asking people in my neighborhood, many of whom follow voodoo, if they knew Mr. Bokor. One of my neighbors, a busybody from Port-au-Prince, said that she knew him, and that I hated him because he turned my brother into a zombie. The police, they don't believe in zombies, but they believe I hated Mr. Bokor."

"By the way, where is Carl?" I asked.

"I told him to stay home. He has been very agitated lately."

"Why?"

"Because of the murder, of course. And because the police made me visit them."

"Did he hate Mr. Bokor, too?"

She nodded. "He never volunteered to be reanimated."

"Is everything straightened out with the police?" Luisa asked. "Will they stop bothering you?"

"I told them my brother remains dead, which is technically the truth. I said I wasn't angry at Mr. Bokor, but I didn't approve of sorcerers. And they admitted that all they had was the one neighbor's claim. Best of all, I have an alibi. After I left the botanica that night, I was at home cooking and serving dinner to my daughter and grandchildren."

"That's a relief," I said.

"It was a waste of my time."

"Absolutely," Luisa said.

After a moment of awkward silence, Madame Tibodet spoke.

"Yes, I'm glad that foul man is dead. He brought down upon him the wrath of the loas."

More awkward silence. The bells above the door saved the day as a woman entered the store.

"Ah, my client is here. Josephine, come with me to the back room."

To be honest, Madame Tibodet made a good suspect in my eyes, but there were better ones.

Matt called me regarding one of them.

"I keep thinking of the realtor," he said, "and all the money he lost in that big real estate deal that never happened. So, I was poking around online in the county's public records and found something interesting. Brad Keeble took out a second mortgage on his house shortly before the deal dissolved."

"And he told us he gave his retirement savings to Mr. Bokor."

"Yep. No one knows what Mr. Bokor did with all this money, but Brad didn't get it back. Can you imagine how it felt to explain that to his wife? He has kids, too."

"In other words, he had a great motive to kill Mr. Bokor."

"Exactly."

"I searched the property appraiser's website to see what other real estate Brad owned. I figured he'd have a bunch of properties in the process of being flipped. But he doesn't. There's only the house he bought with his wife and a condo he recently bought under his own name."

"Why only his name?"

"I don't know. He could be having marital problems. Who knows? Anyway, my guess is that the condo is a rental property to bring in extra income. I drove by there to see if I could talk to the tenant, but no one was there."

"Whose name is on the homes Mr. Bokor bought to flip?"

"Mr. Bokor's only."

"That means all Brad got for his work was inflated commissions, and all he got for his investment in the development deal was a big fat zero."

"Exactly."

"Is he on Shortle's radar?"

"He is now. I shared with her everything I found out."

"Too bad our police department is so lacking."

"It's a small city where murders are rare," Matt said. "I'll give her a pass for not being as conspiratorially minded as you and I are."

"Is that what binds us? Conspiracy theories and dubious monster legends?"

"Yep. And that cafe on the beach."

"We have sarcasm in common."

"That, too. Anyway, I called Brad and asked if we could meet with him. I made sure it didn't sound like we suspected him."

"Did he agree?"

"He said he'll be going into the office early tomorrow. He'll make time for us at seven."

"I'll meet you there in the parking lot," I said. "You bring a recording device, and I'll bring my truth spell."

"Good thing no one believes in magic. If he confesses under the influence of your spell, we want it to hold up in court."

"I just want to know if he was the murderer."

Of course, things are never that simple.

CHAPTER 13
EARLY MORNING MEETINGS

This time of year, it was still dark at 7:00 a.m., and the building that housed the Jellyfish Beach Executive Suites had horrible lighting in the parking lot.

It was so horrible that I almost missed the horse galloping by.

"Did you see that horse?" I asked Matt.

He stopped his pickup truck in the middle of the parking lot.

"I did. In fact, I think it was Trevor, the centaur."

"Go after him! He was headed for the street."

Matt lost his stunned expression and hit the accelerator, his rusty vehicle lurching out of the lot onto the main road. Fortunately, traffic was sparse around here at this hour.

I caught the flash of a white horse's tail disappearing around the corner of a bank next door.

"There he is!" I pointed. "He's going past the drive-through window."

Matt pulled into the bank parking lot and went around the building, tires screeching. When we entered the drive-through lane, the horse was already racing through a gap in a hedge into the small shopping plaza next door. He wore a jacket on his human half, which made the sight even more bizarre.

We couldn't drive through the hedge, so I jumped out of the truck and told Matt to meet me in the plaza's parking lot.

Cutting through the hedge, almost slipping on horse poop, I sprinted after the centaur. The parking lot was empty except at the far end, where a yoga studio was the only business open right now. I prayed he wouldn't invade the studio and hurt anyone.

No, he simply thundered past it.

And then, he headed for a bagel shop across the street.

This could end badly, I thought. Dawn was breaking, and more people were starting their morning routines. Any moment now, the centaur would be sighted by someone.

An elderly man was exiting the bagel shop. The centaur galloped straight toward the door. Was he going to go inside? I imagined complete pandemonium.

But the creature turned sharply left and charged past the elderly man, almost knocking him over. I crossed the street and caught a last glimpse of the centaur. He had the man's bag of bagels in one hand.

"Are you okay?" I asked the flustered man.

"Why is a horse loose in downtown Jellyfish Beach?"

"He was hungry," I said and resumed my dash after the centaur.

I wanted a chance to talk to the creature and ask him about the murder of Mr. Bokor. I also wanted to ask why he'd been in

Bokor's office the other night. And what was he doing there again this morning? But now, I was more concerned that people would see him.

A clatter of hooves made me turn just in time to see the centaur race from an alley toward the street. In front of him, a landscaping truck sat idling at a red light. With equestrian agility and grace, the centaur leaped high in the air and landed in the back of the truck. It drove away when the light turned green, the driver apparently unaware of the creature catching a free ride.

I stood on the sidewalk, shaking my head in wonder, when Matt finally pulled up.

"Did you lose him?" he asked through his open window.

"He jumped into a landscaping truck. I hope he can get out without being seen."

"He seems quite adept at it, not counting you and me."

When I got into the cab, I asked Matt why the centaur would have returned to the office.

"It can't be a coincidence," he replied. "He must have wanted to get back into Mr. Bokor's office again for some reason."

"I agree." I glanced at my watch. "We're late for our appointment with Brad. I wonder if he saw the centaur?"

The rising sun bled around the edges of the building as we parked and went into the lobby, which didn't require a key card at this time of day. We took the elevator to the second floor. The front door of the executive suites had been left unlocked by Brad.

"Hello?" I called out from the reception desk.

No answer. Matt and I started down the hall toward Brad's office. Every door was closed except for his. Light poured out.

My nose was assaulted by unpleasant smells. Was that manure? And there was also a sickening coppery scent.

Just before we reached Brad's office, I saw the horse manure in his doorway. The centaur had been here.

The coppery smell was intense now. I felt nauseated, along with a sense of dread.

Careful not to step on the poop, we stood side by side in the open door.

"Morning, Brad," Matt said.

Brad was at his desk, but his chair had been turned to face the window, so only the back of his head was visible.

"Did you see the, um, animal?" I asked.

Brad did not reply. The dread was overwhelming me.

Matt and I hesitated, neither of us wanting to enter the office, but I went first.

"Brad, are you okay?"

At this point, I knew he wasn't going to answer me. I walked around his desk, hoping, beyond reason, that he was asleep. And knowing in my gut that I was about to see something awful. My gut was correct.

Brad reclined in his chair, dead. An ice pick or similar tool had done a job on him, and I turned away quickly.

Matt, who had come around the other side of the desk, gasped.

"Looks like he got the same treatment as Mr. Bokor," he said. "Do you see the weapon anywhere?"

"No." I returned to the front of the desk, where I didn't have to see Brad anymore.

"I'm going to assume the centaur did this. And killed Mr. Bokor, too. I can see why he would want to kill the sorcerer who created him if he was bitter and alienated about being a freak of nature. But why would he kill Brad?"

"Maybe it was only because Brad saw him," I said in a thick, woolen voice as I tried to calm my heart and ease my stomach.

"Why would he bring a weapon here?"

"To kill anyone who saw him, I guess. He's a centaur, remember?"

"I guess he hid the weapon in his jacket."

I left the office and stepped over the horse manure in the hallway. It felt good to get away from that scene. Pulling my blouse sleeve over my hand, so I wouldn't leave fingerprints, I checked Mr. Bokor's doorknob across the hall. It was locked. The centaur could have done whatever he needed to do in there —feed the snake again or search for something—and locked the door behind him when he left.

"Can you see any bloody hoof prints in here?" Matt asked.

Reluctantly, I returned to Brad's office and studied the generic gray carpet.

"Nope. He was very careful."

An ear-splitting shriek made me jump.

Eva, the receptionist, stood in the office doorway.

"We just found him," Matt said. "We were supposed to meet him here at seven."

"Is he... dead?"

"Yes. Did anyone else know he was coming in early today?"

"I don't know," she replied, her breathing quick and shallow, as if she were about to hyperventilate. "He comes in early a lot."

"Does he leave the front door unlocked?"

"Yes."

I put an arm around her and led her from the office. Her hair hadn't dried yet from her morning shower and smelled of bergamot.

"Could you please call nine-one-one?" I asked, to keep her mind occupied. "We discovered him right before you arrived and haven't called yet."

She nodded and headed to the front desk.

I stayed outside the office. There was no way I would go back in there.

"You know, there's still the chance your theory is correct," I said. "Brad could have killed Mr. Bokor over money. And then Trevor came here to get something from Mr. Bokor's office and killed Brad after being seen. Or the centaur knew Brad killed his maker and came here to search Brad's office or to get revenge."

"Either way, we'll never hear Brad's side of the story."

"No." A horrible thought occurred to me. "Do you think we'll be suspects in Brad's murder? I guess it looks bad from Eva's point of view."

"Well, we don't have a motive. There could be a security camera in the lobby. It would show we arrived after the time of death."

"I doubt they can pinpoint the time of death to the exact minute. I don't think Brad was killed long before we got here. We saw the centaur leaving, after all."

"And the camera would show the centaur. That's not good. Let's hope there isn't a camera."

Matt sighed. "Nothing about this is good." He left the office. "We should see if Eva knows anything."

"I'll talk to her. You can stay here and look for clues."

"What clues? I'm not a forensics expert."

"Maybe the killer dropped something. Like the weapon."

I walked away from him, hoping he wouldn't follow. No need for him to flirt with Eva. I reached the front desk to find her sitting with her elbows on her desk and her face in her hands.

"Are you okay?" I asked in my tender, nursing voice.

"I never saw anyone who was murdered before." She removed her tear-streaked face from her hands. "It's terrible. And Brad was a nice guy. And this, right after poor Jules."

I thought she hadn't liked Mr. Bokor.

"Do you have any guesses as to who would do this?"

"Maybe it had something to do with their secret real estate deals."

"What deals?" I asked, feigning ignorance. In my pocket was the powder I used with my truth spell, but it seemed cruel to use it on her now.

"There was some big development project that Jules and Brad were planning. They tried to keep it a secret from me, but I overhear way more than people realize. The project never happened. There were other investors. The mob could have been involved, for all I know."

"Do you know the names of the investors?"

"No. Sorry."

That was a topic we'd been planning to ask Brad about. My truth spell would have gotten specific names.

"There's one thing that doesn't make sense," Eva said. "Why is there manure in the hallway?"

"I don't know," I lied. "It could be a symbolic thing the mob does when they whack someone. To send a message."

"That's horrible. It's disrespectful to the victim."

"That's the point."

Matt sauntered up to the desk. "Are you all right, Eva?"

"I'm struggling. Thank you for asking."

She smiled at him. This was no time for smiling, not with a dead guy down the hall.

I was about to tell Matt about the mob theory when the door opened, and Shortle walked in, followed by a uniformed female officer. Shortle did a double take when she saw me.

"*You*? You're on the scene of another murder? Did you discover the body?"

"Well, Matt and I discovered it together."

"You're supposed to be a kooky woman who works in an occult shop. But I think you're the Grim Reaper."

"I thought we were becoming friends, Detective."

"I don't have friends, just headaches. Do you realize that not long ago, Jellyfish Beach went five years without a single murder? Now, I can't turn the corner without bumping into you and a stiff."

"It's like the murder rate went up when you started working here."

She swallowed a laugh and scowled at me instead. I felt like I had scored a point, though.

She and the officer went to Brad's office to see the body. Later, Shortle returned to the front desk alone.

"Now, can the three of you give me a summary of what happened?" she asked. "I'll interview you individually when the crime-scene techs get here."

We took turns tossing out details of what we experienced when finding the body. I made sure to mention the completely unsubstantiated theory that the mob was involved and brought it up again when Shortle asked about the manure.

Matt and I, of course, mentioned nothing about the centaur. You can accuse us of being dishonest or withholding information from the police. But that's a fundamental ethos we were forced to adopt after we encountered the supernatural world.

Law enforcement and science do not mix well with the supernatural. People in those fields cannot and will not accept the murky, fantastical world of magic, monsters, and the occult. Telling Shortle about the black-magic rituals behind the church defilements was as far out there as I could go.

Besides, I was now contractually obligated by the Friends of Cryptids Society to protect the secrecy of monsters.

But what if the centaur turns out to be the murderer, you ask?

If the police did, in fact, discover this, the centaur would not get a fair trial. He would be extrajudicially executed by the police. That's what the few of them who encountered monsters have done. I saw it happen to a werewolf once. It happened to my ex-husband, who had become a vampire.

Anything to keep the public from finding out there are monsters in our midst. If people knew about them, there would be civil unrest and deaths that would make the Salem witch trials look like innocent fun.

Despite how we think of ourselves, humans are not rational creatures. Exposure to the completely irrational world of the supernatural activates our lizard brains, and we regress to be like our primate ancestors who lived in constant fear of being eaten.

At least no one was eaten in these murders, if you want to look at the bright side.

The crime-scene techs arrived and went straight back to Brad's office. The younger of the two guys smiled with excitement.

"This is my first murder," he said.

Shortle rolled her eyes, then invited me to the conference room, shared by the tenants of these suites, and forced me to recite everything I had already told her. She was probably hoping to expose an inconsistency. But I think I bored her instead.

A couple of hours later, Matt and I finally left the building.

"What do we do now?" I asked.

"Try to learn who the other investors were. And find that freaking centaur."

After we gave our statements to Shortle, Matt and I drove to our usual beachside cafe for brunch. I hoped it would lighten our moods. It didn't. I don't know about you, but finding dead bodies isn't great for my appetite.

We picked at our food silently, staring across the street at the beach, until Matt perked up.

"We should speak to Brad's wife," he said with conviction.

"Why? That would be so awkward."

"Our theory that Brad was the murderer has been compromised."

"Not if you buy my theory, that Brad killed Mr. Bokor, and Trevor killed Brad, either for revenge or because he'd been seen."

"We have too many theories and not enough facts. New information might point us in another direction."

"I'm sure Shortle already spoke with Brad's wife."

"Yeah, and Shortle isn't sharing any information with us. We're on our own."

"Are we competing with her to see who can solve the murders?"

"Yes," Matt said, spearing a piece of melon. "We're too far into this case now to give up and hope the bumbling Jellyfish Beach Police Department will prevail."

"Wouldn't Brad's widow prefer to be left alone?"

"Of course. But her husband died a violent death. I've had to interview the families of murder victims before. It's not fun for them or for me, but it's necessary."

"Then," I said, "I'll let you set up an appointment and ask the questions."

"There will be no appointment. She would just refuse to meet us. We're going to show up at their home."

I simply didn't have the thick skin required of a journalist. But dealing regularly with vampires, werewolves, and other monsters proved I was not a pansy. Right?

ANGIE KEEBLE ANSWERED the front door wearing a yoga outfit. She was surprisingly attractive to be married to a dweeb like Brad—not to think badly of the dead. Sorry.

"Yes?" she asked, frowning.

"May we take a brief moment of your time to ask a couple of questions about your husband? Sorry for your loss. I'm Matt Rosen, and this is Missy Mindle, from The Jellyfish Beach Journal."

"I was about to leave for yoga class."

"Oh. At a time like this?"

"It's best to stay active when coping with a tragedy," she said.

"Yes, I suppose you're right. I'm sure the police asked you this already, but do you have any thoughts about who might have done this?"

"An officer showed up to give me the news, but no one has asked me any questions. My thoughts about who killed him? Why, I don't know. He was involved in all sorts of sleazy business affairs."

"Real estate ventures?"

"Yes."

"Are you aware of a project with a guy named Jules Bobideau? He also goes by the name Mr. Bokor."

"Of course I'm aware. Brad blew our life savings and took out a second mortgage on the house for that deal," she said angrily. "And lost it all."

I made a note of her reaction.

"We're trying to find out if there were other partners in that venture," Matt said. "Do you know?"

"I don't. Brad was very secretive about it. He was secretive about a lot of things. Like his girlfriends."

"Really?"

"My husband had difficulty keeping his pants on."

"Do you know who these women are?"

"No. I just know they kept him busy."

I couldn't let this go.

"Where were you early this morning, before seven?" I asked.

"I was here in bed."

A muscular man in tight-fitting clothing appeared in the door and gave Angie a deep kiss.

"See you tomorrow," he said.

When he left, he didn't so much as glance at Matt and me.

"Who is that?" Matt asked.

"Claude, my personal trainer. He can supply an alibi for me all morning."

"Thank you for your time, Mrs. Keeble," Matt said. "We'll let you get on with your grieving."

"That didn't get us any worthwhile information," I said as we drove away.

"Except the girlfriends part. Though, I have to admit that Brad didn't seem like the type."

"There isn't a type of person who cheats. There are simply people with a lack of character."

"So, if Brad's wife didn't kill him, then the obvious suspect is Trevor, the centaur," Matt said. "We saw him fleeing the scene, after all."

"I thought you said we were too caught up with theories."

"I did. But it's easier to theorize than to solve this."

"Speaking of theories, I wonder if Eva's suggestion that the mob was involved is worth checking out."

"In all my years of covering Jellyfish Beach, I've seen no mob activity here. A drug lord, yes, but not a criminal gang. But we can't rule out Mr. Bokor raising money from the mob in Miami or Orlando. It just doesn't seem likely to me."

"I'd rather deal with chimeras than the Mafia."

"Me, too. And we still have one to track down."

CHAPTER 14
SHIFTING DISFUNCTION

Discovering dead bodies and being interrogated by the police changes your perspective. The mundane aspects of your life become much more appealing. For me, it meant I gladly immersed myself in my work at the botanica and with home-health visits. Well, at least until a future development in the murder cases makes my life chaotic again.

I knew, of course, that these occupations, despite being mundane, always had a touch of the bizarre. We had a zombie visiting our shop regularly, along with a host of oddball characters, including the guy who came by today. His occupation was wearing a chicken suit and flashing promotional signs outside a nearby fried-chicken restaurant. He was convinced he'd caught the avian flu and wanted a potion to cure it.

Then there was my home-health nursing. How mundane could it truly be to care for werewolves, vampires, and the occasional troll? Measuring pulse rates and oxygen levels was kind of boring, but not when your patient was undead or capable of sprouting fur and turning into a beast during your appointment.

In the case of Harry Roarke, his inability to turn back into a human was a serious challenge for me. As was his resulting nasty mood.

"If he snaps at me one more time, I'm leaving," I said to Cynthia as I held a stethoscope against wolf-Harry's furry chest.

"Here, sweetie, occupy yourself with this."

Cynthia handed him his beloved rawhide bone, which he happily gnawed upon. I was careful to stay clear of his mouth.

"We need to determine if his problem is medical or magical," I said.

"I don't understand why this would happen either way."

"Being a shifter is a supernatural trait, of course. But the body has mechanisms to bring about the physiological transformations. They require hormones from various glands. There could be an infection or other malady blocking that process."

"I see. How on earth can we cure it? Doctors never have to deal with this problem."

"Not directly. But maybe there are treatments for equivalent disorders in humans."

"Equivalent? There's nothing equivalent to turning into a wolf and back again."

"I mean endocrinological disorders. They would present totally differently."

"Obviously. What if this illness permanently took away his ability to shift? I'd be stuck with a wolf for a husband for the rest of my life."

Harry growled.

"I love you no matter what form you're in, sweetie, but we'd never be able to go out to dinner again."

"There are some outdoor cafes where you can bring your dog," I said helpfully. "They even give you a water bowl."

Harry growled.

I forgave his testy mood and Cynthia's bitter sarcasm because they were going through immense stress.

"The other possibility is a witch hexing or cursing him. After all, some people become werewolves because of a curse."

"Not Harry. He was bitten and infected by a werewolf. Same with me."

"I know."

"Who would put a curse on him?" Cynthia asked.

"I don't know. The people who abducted him?"

"But they wanted him to shift back to human, so they'd know for sure he was a werewolf."

"True."

I wondered if my mother had anything to do with it. But I doubted Harry was ever on her radar.

"Harry, did you encounter any humans in the woods before the Knights Simplar attacked you with the silver throwing star?"

He replied in his garbled English. I looked at Cynthia for her translation.

"No. He said he didn't. He smelled the fanatics tracking him for quite a while. He figured they were illegal hunters and tried to avoid them, but decided to circle back on them. They carried a large net, and he realized then that they wanted to catch him alive."

"Ah, so they hoped the throwing star would wound but not kill him, like a silver bullet would," I said.

Harry whined in affirmation.

"You never had any problems shifting before that night?"

He shook his head, slobber flying.

"How would they know a werewolf was in those woods? Do you go there regularly?"

Harry replied. I picked up the word, "park." Unless it was actually, "bark."

"Yes, he goes there all the time," Cynthia said. "There's a lot of natural land there, between the wildlife sanctuary and the state park. He drives there and leaves his car on the side of the road. He thinks someone must have seen him shift as he entered the woods on an earlier occasion, and they monitored the area, looking for his car again."

"That sounds like something the Knights Simplar would do," I said. "It was just bad luck that they spotted you."

"Isn't that a stretch? How low are the odds that they, of all people, saw him?"

"Not as low as you think. Their mission is to wipe out monsters, and they're always on the lookout for them. If you're hunting werewolves, that area is the best place to look within an easy drive of Jellyfish Beach."

Harry growled. I didn't blame him.

"So, what comes next?" Cynthia asked. "How are you going to cure him?"

Good question. I didn't have the expertise to diagnose if he had an endocrinological disorder. I knew of only one doctor in Jellyfish Beach who treated supernaturals, a guy who lost his medical license years ago. But he wasn't an endocrinologist.

"As a witch, I want to begin by seeing if I can detect a hex or curse. I hope that's the cause, because I would have a fighting chance of eradicating the harmful magic. Otherwise, I know a doctor I can bring in."

"Has he ever treated something like this?"

"I don't know." Which was true, but I suspected he hadn't. "Can you and Harry come to my house tomorrow night? I'd rather do it there, where I have all my supplies and plenty of room."

And I also had the ghost of a wizard and my iguana witch's familiar to help me.

"I suspect his problem was not caused by a disease or a hex," I said. "I think the silver in the throwing star somehow set off a reaction in his body. If so, I believe my magic can cure it."

We set a time, and I said goodnight. I had a meeting to attend next door at Squid Tower: the weekly vampire creative-writing workshop.

Eight vampires and I sat on folding chairs, arranged in a circle in the community room. I smiled at the familiar faces of men and women, physically in their sixties, seventies, and eighties. But some had existed for centuries after they were turned into vampires.

Their minds and personalities were ossified and unchanging. A few of them had improved slightly in their writing craft, but none would evolve into great writers.

Walt Whitman, the famous poet, was the only one with talent. But even he showed no signs of adopting new styles or techniques.

For them, creative writing was just one means of combatting the boredom that came with living for an eternity. And I made a little extra cash by being here to indulge them.

Once in a while, they surprised me.

Marjorie rarely shared her work with the group. In fact, most sessions were dominated by the same few writers, such as Gladys, with her insufferable romances laced with erotica. Tonight, however, Marjorie demonstrated rare literary insight.

"I have a poem," she said, standing. "It's called, 'Too Pretty for this World.'"

It was in free verse. She cleared her throat and recited the lines in an emotional voice.

"My twin daughters, little cherubs, true princesses,
Twenty years old, at the peak of their beauty,
Frozen forever at that age by violence.
A monster not content to sip their sweet blood,
Overcome by the intoxicating taste of youth,
Drained them. And when their eyes fluttered
Closed in death, he turned the girls and brought them back.
Undead, unchanging, undyingly adorable,
They will never become happy mothers of their own,
Or become disappointed by the wreckage of their lives.
They will always be sweet cherubs, cute as dolls,
Innocent, as only the young, and the dead, can be.
I enjoy them during holiday visits,
Reveling in their pure beauty.
Knowing they will never change, never turn against me.

Why do I have the right to enjoy these perfect daughters,

When the monster who turned them,

Had no right to do so at all?"

Then silence. Marjorie gave a small smile and took her seat.

"Brilliant!" Walt Whitman exclaimed.

"Disturbing," Gladys complained. "No one wants to hear about daughters being turned."

"No one wants to hear your personal porn fantasies, either," Schwartz quipped.

Reading the poem made Marjorie all choked up. Doris was weeping openly, blood-red tears streaming down her face.

So much for light-hearted escapism, I thought.

"That was well-written and thought-provoking," I said to Marjorie. "What inspired you to compose it?"

"It's about my own children. They were turned when they were visiting a theme park in Orlando. I had already been turned, but they didn't know it at the time. They would have wondered why they were aging while I never changed."

"I can only imagine the pain vampires feel when they outlive their human children and grandchildren."

Now, Sol was crying, too. I'd never seen the crusty old vampire show any emotion.

"I didn't have to experience the pain of outliving them," Marjorie said. "And I've enjoyed that fact. I've delighted in my beautiful daughters who never lose their beauty and never will. Sometimes, I feel guilty for feeling that way."

The group stared at her, uncomprehending. As I've said before, vampires are predators and amoral in many ways.

"Why would you feel guilty?" Schwartz asked in his rough Brooklyn accent. "You're a vampire, and they're vampires."

"I didn't choose to become a vampire. Neither did my daughters. They'll always be perfectly beautiful, but they'll never be mothers or grandmothers. The monster who turned them—what gave him the right to make them vampires?"

"I've always said that feeding is fine," Lucy replied, "but killing and turning someone is murder, even if your victim isn't truly dead."

"This sounds preachy, I know," Marjorie said. "But humans were created to grow old and die. Vampires who turn them are playing God."

"There are enough vampires in this world already," said Gladys. "If we keep making them, the world will be over-crowded with us."

I totally agreed with her, but kept my mouth shut.

"Your poem is a metaphor for the artist and the act of creation," Walt said.

"And the story of Dr. Frankenstein," Doris added.

"I don't know," Schwartz said. "I never had kids. And I can't have any now. Who's saying I'm not allowed to turn someone, so they'll be my child?"

"Being a maker is not the same as being a parent," Marjorie snapped at him. "It's selfish."

Others grumbled in agreement.

Never had the literary works from this seminar ever enlightened me or paralleled my life, but this poem did.

Mr. Bokor had given life to creatures that shouldn't exist in order to benefit Igor and himself. He wasn't furthering the human species—or any other species. It was for profit, and it was wrong. It was especially an injustice to make these creatures exist in a world where they didn't belong.

I felt pity for the chimeras, especially the human hybrids. The centaur had no right to murder anyone, but I nevertheless empathized with his plight.

"Can I read my story now?" Gladys asked.

Everyone said yes, eager to change the dark mood in the room.

Even Schwartz seemed happy to hear Gladys's tale of the elderly vampire with her harem of hot pool boys.

Something about Marjorie's story kept nagging me. Not its melancholy air, but something more granular. The idea of twins festered in my brain.

Finally, the reason why struck me. And I was horrified by what it might portend.

CHAPTER 15

PACHYDERM PROBLEMS

"T*wins*?" Matt asked over the phone. "Are you serious?"

"Unfortunately, I am. Remember, Mr. Bokor's magic involved exchanging characteristics between the offspring in the wombs of two different creatures who were in proximity. The cat would then go on to birth a cat-dog, and the dog would have a dog-cat. Kind of like twins that mirrored each other."

"So, you're saying there's another centaur out there who's a different degree of horse-like than the one we've encountered?"

"Yes, possibly," I replied. "More or less homicidal than our guy. Same with the elephant."

"Let me try to talk you off the ledge. So far, the only people murdered have been Mr. Bokor and Brad. Both were killed in the same fashion. We saw the centaur at the second murder scene. In my eyes, there's only one homicidal chimera, and it's him."

"You don't believe Eva's suggestion that the murders were mob related?"

"I'm open to the possibility."

Or the possibility of him and Eva? I kept my jealous thoughts to myself.

"I'll try to find out more about the investors," he continued, "but it sounds like Mr. Bokor was the one who embezzled the funds. Brad didn't harm any investors, as far as I know."

"Let's ask Igor if he knows more about the centaur than he told us. And we'll ask about the twin chimeras."

"You sure do enjoy visiting Igor." He sounded like the jealous one now.

Before going to bed, I watched the local news. Nowadays, people's TV- and video-viewing habits are all over the place, but I guess I'm old school. I still watch the TV stations located in my local market to learn the news that the cable networks would never carry.

Being friends with a reporter is an enormous influence on that. Folks, you need to support your hometown journalists. I'm a loyal subscriber to *The Jellyfish Beach Journal*, though I admit it's partly because I need something to spread on the garage floor to protect it from Tony's poop.

Tonight's broadcast had a feel-good fluff piece about an escaped elephant that had been returned to the Savanna Safari Park west of Jellyfish Beach. This tourist attraction allows visitors to drive their cars through an imitation

African savanna complete with lions, zebras, elephants, and the like.

I was surprised I hadn't heard about the elephant escaping. I must have missed too many local news broadcasts. It was kind of ironic hearing about an elephant in the area after the hideous experiments creating chimeras.

At the end of the story, the zookeeper was petting the elephant's shoulder when the reporter made a silly joke about feeding the creature more peanuts so he wouldn't escape again.

The elephant turned his head and glared at the reporter as if insulted.

Everyone knows elephants are intelligent, but there was something in his eyes that gave me chills. They had the piercing, insightful stare of a human's eyes. It was uncanny.

And it got me thinking that I had a lot of questions to ask Igor.

"How could I be so fortunate to be visited by such beauty once again?" Igor said, when he opened his front door.

"It's good to see you, too," Matt snarked.

"Your tagalong here is a bit grumpy tonight," Igor said. "Perhaps he'd like a mango smoothie?"

"I'd just like to ask you some questions."

"Then, come along with me to the sunroom where I was lounging."

Why a vampire would lounge in a sunroom was beyond me, but it turned out to be a very cozy room with rattan furniture and a curved wall of windows. The windows were covered by thick drapes, of course.

"What questions can I answer for you?" Igor asked, after sprawling on a loveseat and ottoman.

"We have several," Matt said.

"Go ahead, little man."

Matt's face reddened. I worried he would snap and make a nasty comment. Not a wise move with a vampire.

"The centaur. What more can you tell us about him?" I asked. "We saw him fleeing a murder scene the other day. It was at the executive suites where Mr. Bokor had his office."

"Goodness! That doesn't sound like Trevor at all. Surely, you're not implying that he was the murderer?"

"We're not implying it," Matt said. "We're believing it."

"Oh, no, no. He was Jules' first successful human hybrid and was very close to his creator, and to me, too."

"I beg to differ that any of these hybrids were successful," Matt declared.

"I define successful in that the magic and alchemy worked as planned, producing human-animal hybrids."

"We'll debate the propriety of that another time," I said. "The current situation is there is a dead realtor who was involved with Mr. Bokor in the failed real estate venture—the one in which you lost a lot of money."

"Why are you suggesting Trevor killed him?"

"One theory is that the realtor killed Mr. Bokor because he lost his life savings in the deal. Trevor, then, killed the realtor in revenge. The other theory is that Trevor came to the suites to search for something in Mr. Bokor's office. The realtor saw a living, breathing centaur in the hallway, so Trevor killed him to prevent this knowledge from spreading."

"I find both scenarios preposterous. Trevor is a sweet, gentle creature."

"He escaped his home and now has to survive on the streets without being spotted. How does he find food and shelter? The stress and discomfort could turn anyone violent."

"Does Trevor know about the failed real estate deal?" Matt asked.

"I don't know. As I said before, he was very close to Jules. I wouldn't be surprised if he knew. He has full human intelligence."

"We have a third theory," Matt said. "That Trevor killed Mr. Bokor."

Igor snorted. "That's ludicrous. Why would he do that?"

"Resentment over being created as a freak who will never find a mate or be accepted in society."

"I'll repeat myself. Trevor is sweet. He's not the type to harbor resentment."

"None that you know of. You say he has full human intelligence, but you don't know if his mind has disorders that developed over time. There's no other creature like him in the world."

"The centaurs of mythology were not exactly sweet and cuddly," I added.

"I'm afraid you are trying to make me agree to theories I simply can't accept. This is a waste of our time."

Okay, then I would change the subject.

"You described Mr. Bokor's process for creating chimeras," I said. "Each one had a mirror-image twin, so to speak. The cat-dog had a dog-cat complement."

"I suppose you could put it that way."

"Then what about the human hybrids? Does Trevor have a half-sibling who's more horse, or more human, than he?"

Igor appeared uncomfortable. "No, he doesn't."

"Please explain."

"Jules' technique was concerning to me. I didn't like the thought of a human mother delivering a hybrid. It would be both physically and psychologically damaging. Perhaps, even fatal. Fortunately, I didn't have to worry about that."

"Please explain."

"The human mothers delivered normal, healthy human babies. Their genetic blueprint was transferred to the baby animals, but not vice versa. You could say the magic and alchemy failed to work on humans. I was relieved."

"By the way, who were these human mothers?" Matt asked. "What kind of person would take part in such an experiment?"

"They had no choice but to agree. I mesmerized them."

This whole affair kept getting more disturbing with every fact I learned.

"What about the human-elephant hybrids?" I asked.

"The same result. The elephant delivered hybrids, and the human delivered a normal baby."

"You said 'hybrids' in the plural."

"Yes." Igor cleared his throat. "We didn't realize the mother elephant had been pregnant with twins."

"So, there's another elephant-human hybrid out there?" Matt asked.

"He's being well cared for. I donated him to the Savanna Safari Park."

"Why didn't you tell us about him?"

"He's almost completely an elephant. The average person would have no idea there's any human DNA in him. And, frankly, it's no one's business. I didn't want the Friends of Cryptids Society to bother him. Let him live in peace."

"Did you know he escaped?"

Igor was genuinely surprised. "No."

"You need to watch the local news. He was recently found and returned to the park. He looked like a normal elephant."

"Exactly. Unlike Pete, who is more human than elephant, Percy looks like he's one hundred percent elephant, tusks and all. But he's not. We discovered his brain has human qualities. To be more precise, human intelligence."

"It must be a nightmare to be trapped in another creature's body."

"Not at all. His sense of self is that of an elephant. He simply has the reasoning abilities of a human."

"You sound awfully close to him," Matt said. "Do you two keep in touch?"

"I assume you're being sarcastic."

"No. I'm just curious about how close you are to this creature. Why don't you keep him here?"

"Do you realize how much food elephants eat?" Igor sounded defensive. "And how much they defecate? They can be very destructive, as well."

"Even an intelligent one such as he?"

"Yes. It's the nature of an elephant."

"They can kill with their tusks, can't they?"

I wished Matt would tone it down. I knew where he was going, and it was risky.

"Of course. And they can stomp you to a pulp."

"If you ordered Percy to do so?"

"What are you implying, little man?"

"I'm just thinking aloud. It occurred to me that the two murder victims had wounds made by a sharp, round object. Like an ice pick. A Phillips-head screwdriver. Or, who knows, elephant tusks?"

Personally, I had a hard time imagining an elephant getting its head into the window of Mr. Bokor's car to impale him with its tusks. I could see the elephant's trunk grabbing the sorcerer and tossing him in the dumpster. But regarding killing Brad, could an elephant even fit through the doorways of the office?

"We've already established that I bear no ill will for losing my investment in the real estate scheme," Igor said in a weary, condescending tone.

"You've stated that," Matt replied, "but didn't establish any facts."

"Killing Jules and his business partner wouldn't have achieved anything."

"Retribution—that's what it achieved."

Igor stood. "Enough of your irresponsible accusations. I'm afraid I must ask you to leave now."

I stood.

"Not you. Just the little man."

"We'll both be going," I said. "We've imposed too much on your time and hospitality. Thank you for answering our questions."

"You, my dear, may ask me questions anytime."

In the truck, I scolded Matt for his rudeness.

"It would have been nice if you told me first about this theory of Igor ordering the elephant to kill for him, rather than springing it on us like that."

"You would have told me to say nothing to him," he replied. "I wanted to confront him and see how he reacted."

"And you got nowhere."

"There was something odd about the way he spoke of Percy."

"He cares about him."

"It was more than that."

"I thought we agreed Trevor was the most likely suspect," I said. "Besides, I don't think an elephant can fit inside Brad's office."

"I want to visit the elephant."

"Why? He's intelligent, but he can't answer questions."

"I want to feel his vibe. Does he have the vibe of a killer?"

I shook my head. "You're a hard-nosed reporter, not an empath."

"Okay, I want to see him so I can write a fluff piece about his return, like the TV news did."

"That's so not you."

"Okay, I want to see him because I hate Igor and want to find some way to tie him to these murders."

"Well, at least you're honest."

It turned out that lying about doing a fluff piece was the only way to get a personal visit with Percy. Normally, the elephant would roam the savanna with his herd, and you'd drive by along a winding road, hoping the elephants would approach your car. Instead, the staff of the park agreed to keep Percy at the feeding station until we showed up to meet him and take pictures.

Percy was not pleased. Elephants don't have expressive faces like dogs, but their eyes reveal a lot. Percy's eyes said he knew this was another media meet-and-greet, and he'd much rather be out in the savanna with the females.

The marketing/public relations manager was a perky young woman who recounted how clever Percy was to have escaped, and how grateful the entire park family was to have him back.

Matt listened and took notes, but he was much more focused on Percy's "vibe." So was I. I petted him at the top of his trunk and made serious eye contact with him.

I also cast a simple spell that gave me limited telepathic abilities. Did Percy think in a human language—in the English he must have learned from Mr. Bokor and Igor? If not, what were the elephant's thoughts like?

This chick is hot, a male voice said in my head.

I can hear you, I replied mentally.

I wish you were part of my herd, babe.

My name is Missy. Can you please tell me if you know who killed the man who created you?

No, I don't. I didn't know he was dead. And if you're wondering, it wasn't me who did it.

Do you know Trevor, the man-horse?

We were friends when we were young, but then I was sent to live here.

Do you think Trevor could have killed your creator?

No. Trevor couldn't harm any creature. He even felt guilty whenever his tail swatted flies.

Okay, thank you for your help. Let me ask you one last thing. Are you happy being an elephant?

What else would I be? Yeah, I'm pretty happy here. Plenty to eat, and no one trying to kill me for my tusks. I have a better life than the humans who squeeze inside those metal vehicles, that's for sure.

On our way out of the park, Matt said, "I picked up hostile vibes from Percy. I think he's jealous of me. Maybe he likes you."

"Oh, I don't know. He's just an elephant."

"A smart, strong, ten-thousand-pound elephant. Anyway, I didn't sense any murderous intent in him. Only a dislike of me."

"Since when have you been so perceptive?"

"As a reporter, I need good gut instincts. They're not always right, but they've helped me make the right decisions before. With one big exception."

"What was that?"

"My gut didn't warn me to stay away from this case."

Matt called me in the morning, way too early, considering how late we had spoken previously.

I grunted a hello into the phone, the cats on my bed eyeing me angrily for the disruption.

"Holy Moses! Who's calling you so early?" said Tony from somewhere in my bedroom. He was supposed to be sleeping in the garage.

"Can you believe it?" Matt asked.

"Believe what? I was asleep."

"Sorry. I thought you were watching the news. Percy escaped from the park again."

CHAPTER 16
PERCY IN LOVE

"You've got to be kidding," I said. "Percy escaped?"

"Yeah. He somehow made it through the front gate behind a car that was leaving."

"Don't they have safeguards to prevent that?"

"Sure, but he's a smart elephant. Remember, the vibes I felt were hostile, so we need to be vigilant in case he comes looking for us."

"I don't care how smart he is, elephants can't access the internet to search for our addresses. Besides, I didn't get hostile vibes from him. I think he rather liked me."

"Yeah, guys always like you. But please, be careful."

"I will, I will. But we agree now that we're going to focus on finding Trevor, right?"

"Yeah, but I'm also going to try to learn more about the real estate deal. Can you use your locator spell to look for Trevor?"

"If we break into Mr. Bokor's house again and find a possession of Trevor's. I don't know if centaurs have many possessions."

"It's kind of hard when you don't have pants pockets to put stuff in."

"Right. We'll go over there tonight. I've got to get ready for work now."

I rolled out of bed and headed to the window to open the blinds.

"I got a feeling something's out there," Tony said.

He lay on the rug in front of my dresser. My two cats glared at him from the bed.

"I think you're paranoid," I said, tugging on the draw-strings.

The blinds rose to reveal an elephant's face peering into the window.

The cats disappeared in a blink of my eye.

"Woah. What is he doing here?" Tony asked.

"I think he has a crush on me."

"Do you actively flirt with pachyderms?"

I explained Percy's backstory.

"That is perverse, what they did to him. It goes against the laws of nature, I tell ya."

"Kind of like an iguana who talks."

"That's not funny. I'm no chimera. I'm an iguana through and through. My ancestors just happened to have been bred to have vocal cords."

"Magic was involved."

"Well, yeah."

"I'm going to cast my telepathy spell so I can speak to him."

Once it kicked in, I mentally told Percy to return to the safari park.

I don't want to, he replied. *Can't I hang out here?*

This property isn't zoned for elephants. You really should go home. Your caretakers are very worried about you.

I think of them as my captors.

It's not your fault you're in America instead of Africa, but this environment isn't suited for elephants. The park is the closest thing to your natural habitat. My neighborhood has too many people and cars, plus nothing to eat.

There are plenty of cars where I live.

But they just drive slowly by so the people can look at you. The cars can't crash into you like they can here.

I'm sick of people staring at me like a freak. I'm not a freak! Even though I have some human DNA.

You know about that?

Yeah. Trevor told me about what our father was doing.

Did that make you unhappy?

Being treated like an animal makes me unhappy. And the rest of the herd is stupid. There's no one to share my thoughts with. I definitely can't let my handlers know that I'm not normal. I'm miserable there.

Again, I briefly wondered if his tusks had produced the puncture and slash wounds on the victims. Again, I thought it was unlikely.

I'm going to call the Savanna Safari Park and ask them to pick you up, I said. *You can't walk back there in full daylight without getting into trouble.*

No, I'm not going back. I want to hang out with you.

I'm sorry, Percy. You're a nice guy, but I need to leave for work.

I closed the blinds to allow myself privacy while I showered and dressed. Then, I called the safari park and told them Percy was here, giving them my address. But when I opened the blinds again, he wasn't there. I went outside and didn't see him anywhere. It's not easy for an elephant to hide in a suburban neighborhood.

Though I had broken my telepathy spell before my shower, I wondered if Percy was still reading my thoughts and bolted when I called the park. Did he have natural telepathy? That would be interesting. Or scary.

I know this sounds paranoid, but during my entire drive to the botanica, I felt like I was being watched. Constant glances in my rearview mirror revealed no signs of an elephant following me along Ibis Drive or Jellyfish Beach Boulevard. He wasn't plodding along the sidewalks behind me, either.

Not long after arriving at the botanica, I forgot all about him. The store was busy with the morning rush of customers buying potions and powders to ensure success at their jobs today or to put a curse on their bosses. A large delivery of inventory by UPP took hours for me to stock on the shelves.

It wasn't until Madame Tibodet shrieked in terror that I thought about Percy. Sure enough, he was looming by the front door as she and Carl were exiting.

"It's possessed by an evil loa!" she shouted to Luisa and me.

Carl lurched back inside the store and staggered toward the front counter. He went around to the back of it, sending Luisa scurrying out of the way.

What was he doing?

He reached up along the wall, where expensive items were mounted, and my heart froze.

Carl snatched a ceremonial dagger made from obsidian.

He shuffled back to the front door to protect his sister and caretaker.

"The elephant is harmless," I called after him. He didn't appear to hear me.

Through the display windows, I saw him wave the dagger threateningly at Percy. The elephant reared backward and trumpeted in fear. A car stopped, and the driver took a photo of the beast with his phone.

Rushing outside, I urged Carl to stand down.

"The elephant is tame," I said aloud. "He will not hurt you or Madame Tibodet."

Is that dude a zombie? I can't believe I'm being attacked by a zombie. And since when have zombies used weapons?

Yeah, Percy was naturally telepathic. I hadn't needed to use my spell to communicate with him.

"He's not trying to eat your brain," I said. "He wants to scare you away, so you don't hurt his sister."

I wasn't going to hurt anyone. I just wanted to see where you work.

"You better get out of here before the police show up. Because their guns will not be loaded with tranquilizer darts."

Gotcha.

The elephant trotted away with surprising grace and disappeared down an alleyway.

I ushered Carl and Madame Tibodet inside the shop. Carl placed the dagger on the counter and moaned.

"What was that all about?" Luisa asked.

I explained the elephant was one of Mr. Bokor's chimeras and had human intelligence.

"I should have known that black-hearted sorcerer would send a monster to kill me," Madame Tibodet said.

"No, he didn't come here to kill you. He escaped from the Savanna Safari Park and has a crush on me."

Both women and the zombie looked at me in disbelief.

"Yep," I said. "Beauty tamed the beast."

"What does he want?" Luisa asked. "A date?"

"No. I think he just wants to get to know me better."

"And then what?"

"I don't know. I guess I'll have to visit him a lot at the safari park."

"Don't even think of adopting him. You already have two cats and a lizard. Feeding an elephant will bankrupt you."

"Don't worry. He's going to live in the park."

I checked my phone and found ten missed calls and four voicemails. They were from the safari park. They had shown up at my house with a truck for Percy, but he wasn't there.

I called them back and told them where he was last spotted.

"You need to alert the police about him so they don't shoot him," I advised.

"How could an elephant walk all the way from your house to here without raising an alarm?" Luisa asked.

"Beats me. Maybe he's magical."

I said that sarcastically without thinking. But it occurred to me that there might, indeed, be something magical about him, an ability he possessed naturally or a knowledge of how to cast a spell. After all, he was telepathic and could very well be capable of making himself invisible.

You never know in Mr. Bokor's twisted world. Perhaps the

sorcerer had given him special abilities to make him useful as an internet scammer for Igor, despite the fact he had an elephant's body.

As if things weren't weird enough, Mrs. Lupis and Mr. Lopez walked in. I had been remiss in keeping them abreast of what Matt and I had been up to because I'd been too focused on solving murders to catalog chimeras.

"You have not kept us abreast of what you've been up to," Mrs. Lupis said.

"My thoughts exactly. I've been busy. But the only creature I haven't told you about is one I met yesterday. He's an elephant-human hybrid. Outwardly, he's one hundred percent elephant, but he has human, or human-like, intelligence."

"Hmm, we would like to meet him, as well," Mr. Lopez said.

"Technically, he belongs to the Savanna Safari Park, though I hate to use the word 'belong' with a creature of his intelligence. At the moment, though, he's somewhere in town."

"You mean he escaped?"

"Yes."

"He has a crush on Missy," Luisa said.

I blushed. "In a manner of speaking."

"I want to examine this creature before he is recaptured," Mrs. Lupis said.

I asked why.

"We have certain non-invasive techniques that we can't perform in front of anyone who isn't a member of the Society."

"Very productive techniques," Mr. Lopez added.

I shrugged. "I don't know where he is."

"It sounds as if he wants to be wherever you are," said Mrs.

Lupis. "We will stay with you for the rest of the day in case he shows up."

"You're using me as bait?"

"Precisely," they both said together.

"He's super smart and telepathic. He might also have magic of some sort and can probably sense you guys waiting to ambush him. At the very least, he'll be able to smell you like a normal elephant would."

"Not if you distract him enough," Mrs. Lupis said.

"How?"

"By flirting with him," Luisa said.

The two partners nodded.

"I don't know how to flirt with an elephant," I said. "I'm not good at it with humans, either."

"You don't need to be good at it with most guys," Luisa said.

"All of you are weirdos. Can't we let the poor creature have some peace?"

"She has a soft spot for him already," said my business partner, upon whom I wanted to use a silencing spell.

"I don't think he's coming back here anytime soon. I need to ship a few packages at the UPP store. Let's see if he tracks me down along the way."

"He would come out of hiding in the business district?" Mr. Lopez asked.

"This elephant has a knack for camouflaging himself."

So, there I was, driving my beat-up old car along Jellyfish Beach Boulevard, three packages on the passenger seat and two Society agents hiding in the back seat. Traffic was light, and there was no sight of a pachyderm among the palm trees and early-twentieth-century buildings.

I parked in the lot behind the UPP store and brought my packages in through the back door, followed closely by Mrs. Lupis and Mr. Lopez. I guess they had abandoned any pretense of hiding.

While the clerk was weighing the packages, a movement to my left caught my attention. An elephant's eye and part of his face filled the glass door I had just passed through.

I elbowed Mr. Lopez and motioned with my eyes toward the door. He gasped. So did Mrs. Lupis.

Meanwhile, the clerk had no clue an elephant was at the rear door of his store.

After I paid for the shipping, I led the way outside. Percy had disappeared. Before I reached my car, I noticed the curve of an enormous back and flapping ears protruding above a dumpster that wasn't big enough to hide an elephant.

"He's over there," I whispered. It was disconcerting to see him behind a dumpster, bringing bad memories of finding Mr. Bokor's body.

"You must introduce us," Mrs. Lupis whispered.

Percy, I see you hiding back there, I thought, hoping he would hear my words telepathically. *I have two friends I'd like you to meet.*

Are you trying to trick me? he replied in my mind.

No, they're on your side. You can trust them.

His eyes appeared above the rim of the dumpster.

Okay, bring them over.

We three humans went around the dumpster where the elephant towered above us, swinging his trunk nervously.

"This is Mrs. Lupis and Mr. Lopez of the Friends of Cryptids Society," I said aloud. "They study creatures that are not officially recognized by science."

"Mind if I do a reading?" Mr. Lopez asked. "It's pain-free and harmless."

Before he received an answer, he placed his smartphone against Percy's side.

"We have a proprietary app," he explained.

He studied his phone's screen for several seconds, blocking my view of it.

"Interesting," he whispered to himself.

Mrs. Lupis pulled from her valise an instrument that looked like a tuning fork. She touched Percy's trunk with the two prongs of the fork, and her own forehead with the other end. Her eyes closed.

I almost laughed at the sight of my handlers and an elephant behind a dumpster.

"How long have you had your magical abilities?" Mrs. Lupis asked Percy.

My entire life, his deep voice said in my head. Mrs. Lupis nodded, as if she had heard him, too. *I can prevent humans from seeing me. I do that when I'm tired of being stared at in the safari park.*

"What else can you do?"

Play lawn bowling with my trunk.

"No, I mean magical stuff."

I can pass through walls and fences.

"That is very handy." She glanced at her partner. "Mr. Lopez?"

"A GSI of three thousand to just under six thousand," he replied, putting his phone back in his pocket.

"Impressive."

"What is that the measurement of?" I asked.

"You don't have clearance to know."

"Percy, we would like to interview you sometime soon," said Mrs. Lupis. "Would you be willing?"

Yes, but I'm a bit busy now while I'm on the lam. If I return to the park, you can visit me there.

A truck pulled into the parking lot. It was from the safari park. We humans stepped out of the way in case Percy bolted, but he didn't move.

The truck turned around and left.

"We can see you, but they couldn't?" I asked.

Yes. I can target my invisibility to specific people.

"Pretty cool."

You should spend time with me. There are a lot more cool things I can do.

"I'm sure there are, Percy."

CHAPTER 17
SEEKING CENTAUR

The yellow police tape had disappeared from Mr. Bokor's house. His lawn service had, too. The grass was several inches tall, and the house had a forlorn, abandoned look. I wondered if there were any distant family members to inherit the place. Good luck putting it on the market when one of the bedrooms was a stable.

This was the second time Matt and I had broken in, and we displayed the same brash attitude that we had every right to be here, in case a nosy neighbor was watching us from a window.

I used my own house key to pretend I was unlocking the front door, while I cast an unlocking spell.

We stepped inside and were met by stuffy air and the smell of mildew. The electric company must have cut off power, so there was no air conditioning.

The smell of manure also struck me.

"Trevor must have been here since we last visited," I said.

"Do you think he was searching for something, or was he sleeping here?"

We went down the hallway to the room that contained his horse stall. A fairly fresh pile of horse dung lay on the tile floor of the stall atop a covering of straw.

"You'd think with a human brain, he'd know how to use a toilet," Matt said.

"Unless his horse butt won't cooperate."

"Can you use his poop for your locator spell? It came directly from him."

"It likely has very little of his psychic energy. He had no mental or emotional attachment to it."

"Yeah, I wouldn't either."

"Let's see if we can find something better."

The standing desk was bare except for the remote for the TV. I touched the remote and sensed a decent amount of psychic energy. I would use the remote for my spell unless we found something better.

We looked in the closet. It was large, since this was a luxury home, even though this was a guest bedroom. The closet was filled with shirts and jackets on hangers, and no trousers, of course.

A wooden baseball bat leaned against a rear corner of the closet.

"Man, he would be an awesome ball player with his speed," Matt said.

"But where would he play, and with whom?"

I walked to a window and looked out. The backyard, which was on the Intracoastal Waterway, had a batting cage with a pitching machine set up near the swimming pool. It explained why Mr. Bokor had a bag of baseballs in the trunk of his car when I found his body.

"I got my answer. It looks like he did a lot of hitting. Too bad he had nowhere to run bases."

I returned to the closet and touched the bat. It was brimming with energy. I picked it up and showed it to Matt.

"This will be perfect," I said.

"Should we take it to your house to cast the spell?"

"No. I want to do it here. I'm curious about why Trevor came back and if he's staying here. The way the spell reacts will tell me how much energy he's left elsewhere in the house."

We walked to the kitchen, where I removed my supplies from my tote bag. Matt crossed the living room and opened the blinds a crack to peer out, nervous that we would be caught trespassing. I felt it was worth taking the risk.

I knelt on the expensive faux-wood floor to draw my magic circle with a dry-erase marker. My five tea candles went on its circumference on the points of a pentagram. I gathered my internal energies and enhanced them with those of the five elements. Then, I went to work on the spell while I grasped the handle of the bat.

Reciting the words of the spell, I felt the energy rush from me like water gushing from a fire hydrant.

A glowing orb appeared before me, just above the bat. After making a mental connection with it, I put myself into a trance and waited for an image to appear in my mind. I then gave the orb the command, "Go find the soul to which you belong."

The orb rose a few feet in the air and remained hovering there as if it wasn't sure where to go. Then it buzzed around the room like a fly.

First, it went to the bedroom and hovered above the horse stall. Next, it hurtled down the hall to the bedroom that had been used by Mr. Bokor as an office. It roamed around this room, dove beneath the small table against the wall that served as a desk, and disappeared. Soon after, it reappeared and flew from the room before shooting back down the hall to the kitchen. It hovered beside the refrigerator.

I realized Trevor had been here very recently, since so much of his psychic energy remained.

I was surprised where the orb went next: the family room next to the kitchen. It made a beeline to the fireplace, past an oblivious Matt, and hovered inside it.

Finally, it flew into the living room and passed through the glass of a window facing the street.

I remained inside the magic circle and used magic to enhance my connection with the orb as it flew farther and farther from the house. The orb sent me images of different neighborhoods passing below it as it traveled over Jellyfish Beach and then left the city limits, heading west.

Eventually, real estate developments were less frequent. The orb flew over the Morris Wildlife Refuge and then the Savanna Safari Park. Farmland and patches of forests passed below as the orb continued west.

Never had I sent an orb so far from me. I worried I would lose my connection with it soon.

Thankfully, it slowed down and hovered over a property that looked like an equestrian ranch. I memorized the image so I could compare it to a satellite map and identify the exact location.

The orb descended toward an outbuilding that looked abandoned. As I got a closer look, I saw the roof was damaged, probably from a hurricane. The orb dropped through a hole in the roof.

And there was Trevor, asleep in a dilapidated horse stall, illuminated by partial sunlight pouring through the hole in the roof. The horse part of him stood, while his human head rested on his folded arms atop a half wall.

I felt sorry for him, hiding from us, the authorities, and unknown enemies. Tired, frightened, and alone. Even though he was a murderer, I could empathize with him.

Suddenly, he was bathed in shadow. And a giant shape appeared in the image.

An elephant.

Trevor woke with a start, but smiled when he recognized the elephant. Obviously, it was Percy. Trevor spoke with him, nodding at the elephant's telepathic words.

I had a bad feeling that Percy was tipping Trevor off about our interest in him. With all my magic might, I forced the orb to continue to hover, without going to Trevor and being absorbed into his soul. That was the only way I could follow Trevor if he fled.

He did, in fact, bolt toward the barn door. And the orb won out, so determined to return to the source of the energy that had created it.

It plowed into Trevor's chest, and my image went dark.

Trevor was fleeing, and I did not know where.

I broke the spell, aching with disappointment. I would have to cast another locator spell, but I couldn't use the bat, now drained of energy. The TV remote would be my next choice, though it had less energy than the bat, and a new orb would have to travel farther.

Frankly, I was also exhausted. The spell consumed a lot of my own energy, as well as the forces I had harvested from the elements. It wasn't the most complicated of my spells, but it was among the most draining. I needed a rest.

But first, I left the magic circle and went into the office to check beneath Mr. Bokor's desk, curious about why the orb had gone there. Crouching, I saw a square-shaped incision in the drywall just below where the wooden table touched the wall. I reached forward and pried the drywall outward until the square fell to the floor. It was a secret compartment, but it was empty.

The fireplace came into my mind. What had Trevor been doing there?

I left the office and went into the family room, where Matt was seated on a couch, immersed in something on his phone.

"Oh," he said. "How'd it go?"

"I found him on a horse farm, far west of town. But Percy showed up and must have warned him about us. Trevor took off, and I lost contact."

"Bummer."

"The fireplace smells like a fire burned there recently."

"Yeah, I guess," he said, without looking up from his phone.

"My spell told me there's a bunch of Trevor's psychic energy here. That means he was using the fireplace." I bent down and looked inside. "There's a big pile of ashes. Not coincidentally, the orb led me to a secret compartment beneath Mr. Bokor's desk. It was empty."

Matt glanced at the fireplace. "I know some politicians who

burn their incriminating documents. Sometimes, you can reconstruct shredded documents, but not burned ones."

Never say I turn away from a challenge.

"Science can't help us. But maybe magic can."

Matt was fully engaged now. "Really?"

"I said maybe. I don't happen to know a spell that can do it, but I have folks who can help me find one."

"'Folks'? You mean an iguana and the ghost of a wizard?"

"Exactly. I'll work with them when I get home."

I call Don Mateo and Tony my brain trust. I do so somewhat sarcastically, but they don't know that and consider it a great honor. Don Mateo had been a powerful wizard in early seventeenth-century Madrid but became a target of the Spanish Inquisition and fled to the New World. He met his demise when he accidentally summoned a demon to impress a friend.

The spells he recorded in the back pages of a grimoire have increased my repertoire, and he provides sage advice. But when I called out to him in my house, he didn't answer. Ghosts aren't always dependable.

Tony, my witch's familiar, knows a decent amount of witchcraft from previous magicians he served. His greatest strengths are his telepathy and ability to read my subconscious needs and desires. This way, he can point me in the directions I need to go.

"There are ways to turn the carbon of the ashes back into paper," Tony said, scratching his head crest with a claw. The spiky crest reminded me of a Mohawk hairdo on a punk rocker. "I don't know how to restore the words that were written on it. Don Mateo might know more. Back in his time, secret notes and letters were a big deal."

"Don Mateo, we request your presence," I called. "For the fifth time tonight. I'm growing tired of waiting for you."

I stood in the doorway of my bedroom, looking at the lingerie drawer of my dresser. That's where he usually appeared because of his kinky obsession with silk undergarments.

A tumult came from my closet. I opened the door, and his apparition stood there, wearing my home-health scrubs.

"What are you doing?" I asked him.

"A change in routine is good for a spirit."

"Okay. Whatever."

I presented to him the challenge for his spell-crafting ability.

"Ah, interesting." My scrubs fell to the floor of the closet and Don Mateo floated out wearing his usual frock coat and tights. "I know the perfect spell. I learned it from a wizard who worked for the king's spymasters. They needed a way to read secret notes that foreign spies had burned."

"I told ya he would know," Tony said. The two had been acquaintances when Don Mateo was alive, and Tony was working as a familiar incarnated as a King Charles Cavalier spaniel.

"The spell will turn the ashes back into parchment—or paper, in your case. Also, inks can be restored."

"See, I told ya," Tony said, trying to share credit for the solution.

"The question is in what condition are the ashes," the wizard continued. "In the absence of a breeze and in a gentle fire, the ashes will be in a flat condition, similar to the page from which they came. However, if the ashes have been stirred up, you will have great difficulty in reading what was on the page."

"Oops," I said, showing him a plastic container. "I put the ashes in here so I could bring them home."

"Egad! This will be quite a mess."

We went ahead anyway. Don Mateo directed me to a burn-healing spell he had written in the grimoire and dictated revisions and additions to match the spell used by the spymasters' wizard.

The first part of the process was creating a potion to be spray-misted upon the ashes. I kept an excellent supply of magic ingredients in my garage—almost every conceivable herb, spice, powder, mineral, liquid, and organic material a witch would need. Working at a botanica had its benefits.

Once the potion was complete, I executed the spell within a magic circle. After spraying the ashes with the potion, I recited the lengthy incantation prompted by Don Mateo.

You know those little foam balls you soak in water that expand multiple times over? That was what it was like watching the ashes grow into sheets of paper.

The problem was Don Mateo's prediction proved to be correct. The sheets of paper were of various misshapen sizes, and the typed text was a jumble. In some places, it looked like word clouds, while here and there I could find intact sentences and paragraphs.

I thanked my brain trust for helping me and spent the rest of the night trying to decipher the documents.

What I discovered took my breath away.

The attorneys for Igor Stanisloopsky were notifying Jules Bobideau—aka Mr. Bokor—that he was being sued for misappropriation of the vampire's funds. I couldn't make out if the amount was $59 million or $69 million, but it was pretty darn big.

Apparently, Igor wasn't as cavalier about losing money as he had pretended to be. He had some explaining to do.

CHAPTER 18
TRUTH SPELL

"You think Igor is the murderer, not Trevor?" Matt asked when I called him with my discovery.

"Possibly. A vampire's fangs and long, sharp nails could have caused the wounds that we were thinking came from an ice pick or Phillips-head screwdriver. He might have deliberately avoided making the usual puncture wounds in major blood vessels that would point to a vampire."

"Does this mean we have to confront Igor? I don't think that would be good for our health."

"He could have ordered Trevor to commit the murders," I said. "After all, Trevor burned the legal document that put suspicion on Igor. He must have done that under Igor's orders."

"Why would he be subservient to Igor?"

"Igor mesmerized him. How else?"

"It just seems like a centaur is not the best choice for a hired killer. Kind of hard for him to blend into a crowd. Igor could have mesmerized any human to do his bidding."

"Let's have a chat with Trevor. I'll use the TV remote for a new locator spell. Unfortunately, I didn't take it from Mr. Bokor's home. I didn't want to arouse any suspicion in case the police returned and searched the place again."

We agreed to meet early the following morning before my shift at the botanica. I dropped into bed like a stone, exhausted from all my recent spell casting.

I hoped I would be rejuvenated enough in the morning to do it all over again.

Matt and I took separate cars and met at Mr. Bokor's house. It occurred to me that if my spell was successful in locating him, I'd have to call in sick, or send Matt to find Trevor alone. He must be confronted as soon as possible after locating him, to ensure he didn't change locations.

We were both tired and didn't speak as I cast my unlocking spell on the front door. Once it opened, we headed straight for Trevor's room to get the remote.

Only to find Trevor himself.

His human half was looking for something in the closet when we saw him. His horse half reared on its hind legs as he turned to face us.

"What are you doing here?" he asked with both anger and trepidation.

"What are *you* doing here?" I demanded. "We've been looking for you."

"Why? You think I murdered the realtor?"

"Yes. We saw you flee the building and chased you," Matt said. "We found your dung outside his office when we discovered the body."

"Yeah, I know it looks bad, but I didn't kill him. I went there to look for something in my father's office and saw the realtor dead in his office. I panicked and ran away."

"What were you looking for?" I asked.

"Um, nothing."

"Come on, we know all about you. You destroyed a document announcing Igor's lawsuit against your father. Obviously, Igor ordered you to do it. And you were probably looking for additional material in the office that incriminated Igor. Well, it's not in there, because we already looked."

"Why were you following Igor's orders?" Matt asked. "Were you mesmerized?"

"Mesmerized into killing both victims?" I asked.

The way Trevor's eyes darted toward the hall behind us told me he was about to flee. I quickly cast an immobility spell.

He reared on his hind legs again, forcing Matt and me to duck out of the way as Trevor charged past us into the hall.

The spell kicked in before he made it to the kitchen, and he dropped with a clatter onto the faux-wood tiles.

"That was close. Now I know why cops use horses for crowd control," Matt said.

I approached Trevor. He looked up at me in terror.

"What did you do to me?"

"I'm a witch. I used a spell to immobilize you. Next, I'm going to use one to make you tell the truth."

I hate to admit it, but I carry a baggie of my truth-telling powder in my pocket whenever I leave the house. The way our society has devolved, I never know when I'll need to use it.

I sprinkled it on Trevor's torso and recited the invocation. His face lit up with alertness and an eagerness to talk.

"Did you kill Mr. Bokor?" I asked in a neutral voice.

"No."

"Did you participate in any way in his murder?"

"No. I swear to you I didn't."

"Did you kill Brad Keeble or participate in his murder?"

"No. Like I told you, I stumbled upon the scene by accident."

"Why were you at the executive suites? What were you looking for in Mr. Bokor's office?"

"Threatening messages from Igor. He was demanding his investment be returned from a real estate deal. He thought his messages would look bad in light of my father being murdered."

"You realize the police already took his computer to examine it?"

"Yeah. Igor sent them on an app that automatically deletes them. He was afraid that my father had printed them."

"He hadn't. We already searched his office. Is that also why you burned the document about Igor's lawsuit against your father?"

"How do you know about that?"

"I'm a witch, remember?" He didn't need to know how much effort went into deciphering that document.

"Yes," he said. "Igor didn't want the police to see it."

"Did Igor kill your father and Brad?"

"No. I mean, I don't know. He didn't say."

"Do you suspect he murdered them?"

"Look, he's a vampire. He thinks nothing of killing people. I wouldn't put it past him, but he's also not the hands-on type. Except when he's feeding."

"Wouldn't you be angry if he killed your father?"

"I call Jules my father because he created me, though he literally wasn't my dad. I guess I have two real dads: a stallion and a human." He shook his head in shame. Tears streamed from his eyes. "Jules didn't really care about me. He let me live with him and gave me the stuff I needed. Igor was really the one who raised me."

"*Igor*?" Matt asked, aghast.

I glared at him to keep quiet. I had to be the one who asked the questions with this spell.

"How do you mean, Igor raised you?" I asked.

"He homeschooled me and treats me with respect, instead of like a freak. He's given me money after Jules died. Igor has always believed in me and promised to invest in my big dream."

"And what would that be?"

"A tapas restaurant. I want to open my very own place. Being a chef and owner was what I've wanted to do for years."

"A centaur with a restaurant?" Matt asked.

I shushed him.

"I see your friend is one of those people who thinks diversity is a dirty word," Trevor said to me. "But I'm an excellent cook. I'll just stay in the kitchen when customers are in the restaurant. I'll hire discreet staff who will be paid well enough to keep their mouths shut about me."

"And you'll be able to afford to do so because of Igor?"

"Right. He said he'll inject as much cash as it takes for me to succeed."

"That's very generous of him. Igor pretended money meant nothing to him, but he was apparently upset about Mr. Bokor not paying back his investment."

"It was a lot of money. But I think he was more upset at being lied to while Jules spent the money like a drunken sailor on this house, a giant yacht, and a private jet."

"Wow," I said. "That was truly extravagant."

"He left his investors really mad."

"Were there others aside from Igor and Brad?"

"I think so. But I don't know who they were."

I wish I knew how to find out. Matt's research into the failed development deal came up with the name of the shell company Mr. Bokor set up. It was a trust, which made it more complicated to learn who the investment partners were.

"Mr. Bokor hid the lawsuit letter in the secret compartment in his home office. Did he have other hiding spots?"

"Probably. He was sneaky like that. I only knew about the one under his desk because I accidentally saw him using it once."

"Thank you, Trevor, for your candor," I said, even though it was my spell that made him candid. It was beginning to wear off, though.

I was finished with him. I broke the immobility spell, and before I could say a word, he scrambled back up onto his hooves and galloped through the house and out the front door.

"I wouldn't have believed him if not for your truth spell," Matt said. "It appears that Igor is our main suspect now. How in the world can we bring him to justice?"

"We can't allow him to be arrested, but if we get him to confess, I'll feel a small amount of closure."

"But is that justice?"

"Not really. Which is why I'll inform the Society about his crimes. Maybe they'll get rid of him." My mind roved the surrounding walls, as if I could spot another hidden compartment. "Before we deal with him, I want to search this place some more."

I had a spell that recently helped me find the secret hiding place of a computer's external hard drive. This would be the perfect opportunity to use it again. It detects the energy left behind by strong emotions. When you're doing something furtive, such as hiding documents in a secret place, you don't do it indifferently as you would when returning a cereal box to the pantry.

When you're being sneaky, you might have a variety of emotions, from smugness or pride in your craftiness to anxiety or guilt. The other emotions you have each day leave traces, too. The lingering energy from the loving feelings you left on a sofa where you sat beside your partner would obviously not help me find a secret compartment.

I stepped into Mr. Bokor's bedroom for privacy and put myself into a meditative state. I could create this spell without using a magic circle.

Clutching the power charm I carried in my pocket, I gathered my energies. As the power grew within me like water coming to a boil, I recited the incantation.

A sparkling cloud formed around my head. It was subtle and didn't affect my vision, but it lit up whenever I was near energy left behind by strong emotions. So far, I wasn't picking up any at all in Mr. Bokor's bedroom. Frankly, I preferred not to find any related to his personal life. I only wanted to find where he hid stuff.

I checked the bathroom cabinets and the large closet, visually inspecting surfaces for seams or human-made cracks. I scanned the floor, looking for loose marble tiles. When I passed the large vanity mirror, the cloud lit up with multiple colors. Appropriately enough, the emotion I sensed was vanity. Mr. Bokor must have spent a lot of time gazing in the mirror at himself admiringly.

I shuddered at the thought.

Next, I went to the walk-in closet. It made mine at home look like a broom closet. This one even had an island counter in the center with drawers. The closet was largely empty, though, except for a few groupings of clothes on hangers near the door. Mr. Bokor was definitely not a fashion plate.

I paid close attention to the drywall and tiled floor. No signs of hidden compartments. The small throw rug by the door had nothing beneath it. And the cloud around my head was inert.

Searching the entire house was going to take a while, I realized with regret.

As I headed toward the kitchen, my cloud lit up with an urgent, powerful emotion.

It was fear.

Matt hung two feet in the air from Igor's hand that gripped the back of Matt's neck.

"If I sense any magic coming from you, I will pop his head off," the vampire said to me.

I immediately broke my emotion-sensing spell.

"Leave him alone," I said. "What do you want?"

Igor took three long sniffs. "Good girl. No magic, okay?"

"Okay. You can smell magic?"

"In a way. However, it's not my olfactory glands that sense it."

"Will you set him down now?"

Igor lowered Matt to the floor but kept his hand locked on the back of his neck.

"I don't know what to do with you two," Igor said sadly.

"You can let us go home," Matt replied. "Ouch! Don't squeeze so hard!"

"It has come to my attention that you suspect me of murdering Jules and the realtor."

So, Trevor betrayed us. I was not surprised.

"We don't suspect you," I said. "I just find it odd that you pretend you don't care about losing money, then send threats to Mr. Bokor and sue him."

"Perfectly acceptable behavior for someone who was swindled out of sixty-nine million dollars. I'm a brilliant investor in stocks and bonds, but apparently, I'm a blind fool when I give money to a business partner. The insult to my honor bothers me more than the loss of the money. But we vampires live forever, so we can't be too profligate."

"I understand," I said before taking an enormous risk. "Did you kill them?"

"Ouch!" Matt yelled. "That hurt!"

"I did not. And I can't fathom why you'd think I killed the realtor, who was just another victim like me."

"True. But you killed Mr. Bokor?"

"Ow! My neck is not a stress ball!"

"Death was too merciful for Jules. If I had punished him, I would have mesmerized him and made him my slave, so he could earn back a bit of the money he stole."

"Then who killed him?"

"I don't have the faintest idea. I'm completely baffled, as I am about the current situation."

"Um, what do you mean?"

"How do I deal with you two? You suspect me of murder, and your loose lips can cause me serious trouble."

"If you're innocent, you have nothing to fear from us."

"Loose lips, my dear. The only way to guarantee your lips don't talk is to make you my slaves. Or kill you. Which will it be?"

CHAPTER 19
VAMPIRE VEXATION

Matt and I had been mesmerized. Speaking for myself, it was just enough to make me docile, but not as much as if I had been fated to work as a slave in his scam factory. As we sat in the backseat of Igor's vehicle, my brain was independent enough to be bothered by a question.

Why was a vampire driving a minivan? I mean, he was rich, urbane, and a monster—far from a suburban soccer dad. The vehicle was giving me cognitive dissonance. Not that there's anything wrong with minivans. I wouldn't mind having one. But they're like cargo shorts. I wear them, but vampires just don't.

Yes, I know. I was being driven to my possible murder, and I was fretting over Igor's ride? It's called gallows humor, and it's all I had to keep from panicking.

Igor's face appeared in the rearview mirror.

"Are you both wearing your safety belts? I worry about you humans. You're so fragile."

That didn't sound like a vampire who was going to enslave or kill us, but I knew better.

Under this light mesmerization, I couldn't cast a spell to save us. I hoped I'd have an opportunity later if the mesmerization wore off, or if I could calm down enough to gain more control of my mind.

Matt stared ahead blankly, as if he'd been lobotomized. Igor must have mesmerized him more thoroughly than me. Igor was acting like a typical male, assuming a man would be more dangerous to him. This was despite knowing I was a witch.

He obviously didn't realize how powerful my magic was. If only I could use it.

Igor turned into his long, winding driveway, and we passed the cemetery and the skeletons hanging from trees. I would have asked him about the skeletons if I had the energy to speak.

He didn't drive to the front entrance. Instead, he swung around to the rear garage he had converted into the scam factory. He parked near the door.

"Please stay seated," he instructed in a calm voice like a hypnotist's, before getting out of the minivan.

The Missy and Matt I knew would have attempted to escape before the vehicle even stopped moving. Our mesmerized versions wanted nothing more than to stay seated.

Igor opened my door and leaned inside, studying me, then Matt.

"Yes, I have made my decision," he said.

I plunged into unconsciousness.

When I woke up, I was tied to a wheeled office chair. It was one of those expensive brands with the fancy lumbar support. Igor sat in one beside me. Matt was in front of us at a desk in a cubicle. His head moved in jerky, robotic movements as he typed furiously on a keyboard. His workstation had three monitors, and each had multiple windows open. All the major social-media sites were represented across the windows.

"Very good," Igor said in his hypnotist's voice. "You will continue with the friendly banter until you gain their trust."

I leaned forward for a better look. Matt was messaging people via the various platforms.

How are you doing? he typed. *It's been a long time. Don't you remember me? This is Mary.*

"If anyone engages with you, but stops responding, contact them again the next day," Igor told him. "Don't bring up the topic of financial investments until the fifth engagement."

Where do you live now? he typed in multiple windows. *What a coincidence, so do I! Isn't this weather crazy?*

Igor noticed that I was awake.

"Your friend will make a good scam slave. As you can tell, I've restarted operations with all-new slaves. Others are working in the next room, and we're open twenty-four hours. Unfortunately, I must allow them to sleep in between shifts. I'm so disappointed the elephant hybrids didn't work out."

"Please don't make me a scam slave," I said, finally able to talk.

"No, my dear. I envision a much grander role for you."

"As your friend who returns to her house and job, but will always take your phone calls?"

He chuckled. "I am not a wimp like this man you hang out with. You are much too lovely to be only a friend."

Oh, my. What was he proposing? Icy fear spread through my body.

"I'm not interested in dating anyone at the moment," I said in a trembling voice.

"When you become a vampire, you'll feel differently."

"What did you say?"

"I'm going to feed upon you until you're drained. At the exact instant of your death, I will revive you with my own blood, turning you into a vampire. You will be my vampire queen, ruling beside me for eternity as I increase my wealth and power."

I laughed nervously. "You're such a joker."

His face darkened, and he bared his fangs.

"Should I turn you right here in front of your silly little friend?"

My body was frozen, not just with fear but from the mesmerization. Even though mine was lighter than the power that made Matt helpless, I couldn't focus enough to activate any magic.

Missy, girl, you're a witch, I reminded myself. Your powers of concentration are stronger than any normal human's. Magic is in your genes.

Magic is in your blood as it pumps through your body.

Magic is in every breath you take.

Magic rings in your ears.

Magic fills all your senses.

You are magical.

You are magical.

You are magical.

I repeated this mantra, and something shifted in my brain. A film that had been covering it dissolved and fell away.

Finally, I could focus on my solar plexus and feel the heat building as my energies coalesced. At last, my numbed mind became sharper again.

I remembered the incantations. I could visualize the strands of magic that I wove into spells.

Though I was still not completely myself, I began casting two spells. One must follow the other in perfect choreography. It was daunting, but I couldn't allow my difficult odds to lessen my self-confidence.

Self-confidence was critical for a witch to wield power and use magic to affect the physical world. I thought about my mother, and how confident—how arrogant—she was in using her evil brand of magic. Why shouldn't I be even cockier using benevolent magic that was rooted in the power of the earth? And not in demons and death.

Igor caught my eyes. He knew I was up to something. His face was aristocratic and gorgeous, but beneath the superficial beauty lay death. One could argue that vampires weren't inherently evil, but they were indisputably selfish predators that had no benefit to us living creatures of the world.

"Are you trying to cast a spell?" he asked angrily. "You are forbidden to do so."

That undead jerk had no right to tell me what I couldn't do. I would allow him to manipulate me no longer.

My first spell activated. And you wouldn't believe how

relieved I was that it worked. The ropes that bound my arms and legs to the chair dissolved where they touched my flesh, and my limbs were freed.

The second spell kicked in as planned. Igor's eyes rolled up in his head, and he slumped in his chair, snoring.

I leaped up from my chair and shook Matt's shoulder.

He ignored me and continued to type in one of his open windows.

My name is Leslie and I'm 26. I'm looking for a successful businessman.

"Matt, snap out of it. We need to escape now. Igor is under my sleep spell, but it doesn't work for long on vampires."

Matt simply wasn't there. He wasn't even Matt anymore.

I slapped his face.

He looked at me. His expression was slackened, but for the briefest moment, a spark of recognition appeared in his eyes. Then he turned back to his computer, put on a headset, and entered a command that dialed a random phone number.

"Hello," he said. "You have only one week left to purchase an extended warranty for your vehicle."

Matt was unreachable for now. I needed to look after myself and return to rescue him later.

The nearest exit door in the giant converted garage was steel-reinforced and sealed with multiple locks. They would take too much time to unlock magically. I sprinted up a short staircase into the main residence.

Although I'd visited here before, I didn't know what path to take to find an exterior door through the maze of hallways in the sprawling meld of the three homes Igor had transported here. To make matters worse, the hallways ran at odd angles, intersecting with other corridors. All were dimly lit, and the windows were covered with heavy drapes, even though it was night.

I found myself in the sitting room where I'd been before. Igor's cat-dog lay on the couch. The cat head regarded me aloofly, while the dog body wagged its tail with delight. Now, if I could only remember how to get to the front door from here.

Three hallways led from the room. I took the one to the left. It seemed familiar. I recognized the original Monet and Picasso oil paintings on the walls. I believed the foyer was just ahead.

No. I arrived in a formal dining room. The table was large enough for twelve but set for only two. At the end was a giant silver goblet. The seat opposite it had gold-leaf china and silver utensils arranged for a normal human meal.

The only light came from candles in a chandelier above the table and in two wall sconces. The drapes over the windows prevented me from telling which side of the house I was in.

"This is where we will dine, you and I."

Igor stood in one of the two doorways, leaning against the frame as if exhausted. My sleep spell hadn't been powerful enough for him.

"You will be my vampire queen, and all this silly magic of yours will be a distant memory."

I pointed to the elaborate place setting that was for me.

"What's for dinner?" I asked.

"You, my dear."

"My blood cholesterol is too high to be healthy for you."

"Nonsense. Your blood is the sweetest nectar. I can smell it from here."

His eyes grew intense and piercing. The back of my neck

tingled, and the top of my scalp prickled as he attempted to mesmerize me again.

But I was prepared. During our inane bantering, I had placed a protection spell around me, specifically tailored to repel psychic attacks. Igor frowned, realizing his efforts weren't working.

He moved toward me. I retreated to the other side of the table.

The good news: my protection spell was blocking his mesmerization attempts. The bad news: unlike a general protection spell, this one wasn't as effective against physical attacks.

Especially the preternaturally powerful attacks of a vampire.

He leaped across the table at me. I tried to dodge him, but his arm hit my protection bubble and knocked me to the ground.

He crouched above me, baring his fangs, his eyes feral. His urbane veneer had dissolved into a bestial rage. Mouth open, he struck at my neck like a rattlesnake.

Just before his fangs touched my skin, his head bounced backwards, thanks to my protection spell. He growled with frustration.

"Your magic won't stop me for long."

My telekinetic powers, coupled with the same spell I had used to dissolve the ropes that had bound me, severed the chain that held the chandelier above us. It crashed on the table and several candles fell upon Igor.

His cashmere sport coat caught on fire.

Fire is one of the few things besides staking that can kill a vampire. While he screamed and rolled on the floor to damp down the flames, I scrambled to my feet and headed for the doorway.

But a hand clamped around my ankle.

"You will pay for this," he said from the floor, his clothing smoldering.

I don't practice black magic and had no spells to set Igor on fire. Instead, my arm swept lit candles from the table, so they fell upon the vampire. He knocked them away before he caught on fire again.

He stood and smiled at me in a way that nearly stopped my heart. His coat was nothing but charred rags, and his face had burns. But the supernatural healing powers of a vampire made the burns fade before my eyes.

The only remaining light came from two wall sconces with candles. In the corner of my eye was the other entrance to the room, and I sprang in its direction.

Only to find Igor blocking my path.

"Time to die and rise again, my dear," he said in a low, savage voice.

The drapes bulged inward amid the sound of exploding glass. The floor shook as a tremendous object landed.

And through the drapes emerged Percy, the elephant.

He whipped his trunk upward and trumpeted like a battlefield bugle.

Igor stood in shock as the elephant charged him. The vampire avoided Percy's head, but the elephant's shoulder hit him and knocked him onto the table.

Percy pivoted faster than was possible for such a massive creature and charged again.

Igor slashed Percy's forehead with fingernails that had grown inches long. He attempted to leap over the elephant, who reared on his hind legs and snagged the vampire midair with his trunk. He flung him to the floor and stomped upon him before Igor could scurry away, like a cockroach.

Igor's leg was pinned beneath Percy's foot.

"I don't care how big you are," Igor said through clenched teeth. "You can't—"

Percy plunged his head downward and skewered Igor with his tusks. The thrust of his head was fast and savage. Even the preternaturally powerful vampire couldn't avoid it.

One of the tusks apparently punctured Igor's heart. He screamed briefly before his voice faded and died. His body crumbled apart like a burnt log and spread over the floor. It became nothing but dust and empty clothing.

I've never killed anyone before, Percy said sadly in my head. *He wasn't such a bad guy for a vampire.*

"You didn't kill him. He wasn't alive, only undead. You destroyed him, and the world is now a better place. Thank you for saving my life."

Cheered by my words and affectionate pats on his trunk, Percy trumpeted in victory.

CHAPTER 20
SCAM SLAVES

I thought Igor's mesmerization of Matt would have been broken when the vampire was destroyed, but not so. It took about an hour for Matt to return to himself, as if he were recovering from anesthesia.

"What are all these chats and messages on the computer screen?" Matt asked groggily.

"They're all thanks to you, scam slave." I peered at the screen. "Looks like you were in the middle of convincing someone to put his life savings into a crypto account. I'm sure it was secretly owned by Igor."

"I feel dirty."

"It's not your fault. You were mesmerized."

"How did you wake me up?"

"Igor has been destroyed."

Matt's eyes lit up. "No way!"

"Yes. Percy staked him with a tusk in his heart. I was there, moments from being drained and turned by Igor."

"Oh. The two males who love you were battling over you."

"No, the elephant-hybrid who has a crush on me saved me from being turned by an evil vampire."

"Makes you wonder if Percy didn't kill the others with his tusks."

"Don't be silly. We've already discussed this. Igor was the murderer. Stop being jealous of an elephant."

A young man with black hair, wearing shorts and a T-shirt, wandered into the room.

"Who are you?" he asked, looking around with confusion. "And where am I?"

I couldn't tell him that he'd been a prisoner of a vampire, so I fictionalized my answer a bit.

"You were held captive by a cult leader who hypnotized you and forced you to work as a phone and internet scammer."

"You've got to be kidding?"

"No. It's true."

"What a coincidence!" he said, laughing. "I already have my own scamming operation. Why would I be working here?"

"I would say it's karma."

Soon, a dozen other people wandered into the room, men and women from their twenties to forties. They were all disoriented, and when I gave them the cult-leader-hypnotist explanation, they admitted that they, too, had scamming companies.

In the next room were four people on the night shift who sat at their desks bewildered. They had previously been scammers, too.

"You are all free to go home now," I announced. "But let this be a lesson for you. The cult leader who imprisoned you chose you because you were engaged in illegal and immoral behavior. Now is your opportunity to start new, honest lives."

"I've always wanted to make money from credit-card skimming," the first man said.

"The good money is in hacking and ransomware," said another man.

At rare times like this, I wish I had magic that could cause harm.

"You know," I said, "an honest job comes with benefits like a 401K and health insurance. A lot of jobs even allow you to work remotely."

The hum of conversation filled the room as the workers considered this possibility.

"Maybe, I'll sell timeshares," a woman said.

As I walked out of the room, Matt told everyone he wanted to write an article about scam factories.

"Who wants to give me quotes off the record?"

Everyone was working an angle, it seemed. This entire case was about greed and malfeasance. I was just glad that Igor had been stopped, and I could return to my normal life.

It took me an hour and a half to extract Matt from the scam factory so we could go home. Dawn was breaking when the ride-share car I'd ordered picked us up.

"Did you get enough information to write your article?" I asked Matt during the ride.

"Almost. Some of them weren't in the mood to talk, so I'll need to connect with them later. Are we going to report any of this to the police?"

"I'd rather not, because of Igor being a, you know. I'll report everything to the Society and see what they say."

When I was dropped off at home, my handlers were on my front porch waiting for me. As usual, there was no vehicle around.

"We've heard reports a vampire was destroyed," Mrs. Lupis said, without so much as a good morning.

"How did you find out?"

"You should know by now how deeply connected we are with the supernatural community."

"Yes, but no one in the community has found out yet. Except for Percy. Did he tell you?"

"Our sources are confidential," said Mrs. Lupis.

"Okay. Be that way. The sticky part is that the vampire murdered the two humans I've been investigating. How can we put the police investigation to rest without revealing he was a vampire?"

"Simple," Mr. Lopez said. "We say nothing. Let the police resolve it however they decide."

"What if they pin it on an innocent human? I couldn't allow someone to go to jail knowing they were innocent."

"From what you've told us and what we've heard, the only humans suspected were Madame Tibodet, and she was cleared. And the realtor, who was murdered. We suspected chimeras were responsible, but, fortunately, they turned out to be innocent."

"I bet it will end up as a cold case," said Mr. Lopez.

"No one seems to be mourning Mr. Bokor, but Brad had a family," I said. "They deserve closure."

"Not at the cost of revealing the existence of vampires," Mrs. Lupis said.

"So, I'm supposed to say nothing?"

"Yes," they answered in unison.

"Discretion is our motto," Mrs. Lupis added.

"We have a motto?"

It was time to fulfill my much-delayed promise to a friend. And I was ready.

I drew my magic circle much bigger than usual because it needed to accommodate not just me but also Harry, who was a big guy in wolf as well as human form. He sat on his haunches watching me, probably imagining gnawing on my head. Cynthia sat at my kitchen table, observing us dubiously.

Harry scratched himself with a rear paw, threatening to knock over the candle on the upper-righthand point of the pentagram.

I cradled my power charm in my left hand, giving it a direct connection to my heart. Unlike most of my spells, this one would not affect a change in the physical world. Rather, it sensed the presence of magic, disease, performance-enhancing drugs, or high blood sugar. It was a powerful and difficult spell to cast.

Harry growled when I ignited the bowl of incense on the floor between us.

"Good boy," I said. "It won't hurt you."

"He hates incense," Cynthia said. "A reminder of my hippy days."

I touched my finger to my lips to silence her. As the aroma

of sage and clove smoke filled the air, I prepared to sink into my most sensitive, meditative state.

After gathering my energies and those of the elements, I recited an incantation in Latin, Hebrew, and Old English. I threw in a verse of Yoruba just in case Santeria Orishas had been responsible for Harry's plight.

I sat quietly, eyes closed, listening to my breathing. Harry whined, but it didn't disturb my concentration.

Finally, I left my body. And entered Harry's.

My consciousness entered his heart and rode among the blood cells through the rapids of his arteries, down to the tiniest capillaries, and then returned to the heart via his veins.

I jumped from nerve to nerve throughout his nervous system. I crept from gland to gland of his endocrinological system. And I braved the gusty conditions of his pulmonary system. The worst part was enduring a trip through his digestive system. But I had to do it.

I magically traveled through Harry's entire anatomy, searching for disease or ailments, trying to figure out what was preventing him from shifting back to human form.

My perspective was that of a witch, not a doctor. Or, I should say, not a veterinarian. I wouldn't be able to arrive at a medical diagnosis if he was sick, but I would recognize if there was something physically wrong with him.

There was not. Harry was in good health for someone of his age, aside from a bit of hypertension and high cholesterol. This was true regardless of what form he was in. After all, he was still Harry, fur, or no fur.

While I was still magically inside him, I searched for

evidence he was enchanted, hexed, or cursed. And it didn't take long for me to find an answer.

There was a malignant spell affecting, as I had guessed before, his endocrinological system. At first, I thought it might be black magic, but upon studying its energies and how they were woven together, I saw that this was normal magic, albeit of an ancient and primitive kind.

It was time to consult with a specialist.

I set about reversing my spell, and suddenly I was no longer inside the werewolf, but sitting on my kitchen floor staring at him.

Tony, can you hear me? I called in my head, hoping Tony's telepathy would take over. Although the Roarkes obviously knew I was a witch, I didn't want them to know about my talking, telepathic familiar.

Yo, what's up? he replied.

I need you to identify the source of an unusual spell that is keeping my werewolf patient from shifting back to his human form.

I described the unique characteristics of the magic and how its energy was put together.

Definitely Old World, he said in my head. *It doesn't sound like a faerie or pixie created it. My guess is a gnome did it.*

A gnome. That seemed correct. I wasn't fond of gnomes. Three years ago, I had to deal with a spell by my mother that animated the town's decorative garden gnomes and made them go berserk. I had met only two actual gnomes, and they were ill-tempered little buggers.

Cynthia noticed I had opened my eyes. "Did your spell work?"

"Yes. The good news is he doesn't have a physiological problem. It appears a gnome has cast a spell on him."

"A gnome? I didn't know we had gnomes in Florida."

"We do. Not as many as up north or in Europe, but they're here. More of them are moving to the state, just like humans. I guess because we don't have a state income tax."

"Why would a gnome put a harmful spell on Harry?"

"To punish him. Harry must have done something to tick the gnome off. Gnomes like to guard things, like creatures or precious resources. I bet Harry trespassed into the gnome's territory."

Harry growled.

"The gnome could have just warned him," Cynthia said. "He didn't have to harm him like this."

I shrugged. "Gnomes are ornery creatures."

Wiping away part of the magic circle to fully break the spell, I rose to my feet and signaled that Harry was free to leave the circle. He trotted over to his wife.

"Have you seen a gnome or any signs of one?" I asked him.

He shook his shaggy head.

"I need to find this gnome and convince him to break his spell. Show me the woods where you hunt. It's a quarter moon tonight, the optimal time to summon a gnome."

THAT SAME NIGHT, Cynthia drove us in her SUV from Jellyfish Beach to the state park northwest of town. I sat in the passenger seat while Harry was in the back, his head sticking out the window and his tongue flapping in the wind.

I brought with me a bag filled with supplies that were necessary for summoning a gnome. When we pulled to the side of the road and parked beside the trailhead that Harry used to enter the forest, I told them to wait in the car with the windows up. We couldn't allow the gnome to smell Harry's presence and get upset.

Hiking along the trail, I shined my flashlight into the woods on either side, searching for a flat rock, and not just any flat rock. It had to tilt slightly toward the east. The compass in my smartphone confirmed the fourth rock I found had the correct angle.

From my bag, I took a pound of salt, a clump of rosemary, and two coins—one silver and one gold. I placed them on the rock. Next, I opened a can of ale and put beside it a small cake. The last item that was required—and it made me giggle—was a jar of cheese dip.

I recited a short incantation, closed my eyes, and, according to my spell book's directions, cleared my mind of impure thoughts. Not that there were many in there.

There was nothing to do now but wait in the darkness, listening to the wind sift through the trees, the tree frogs chirp, and the occasional small creature rustle the underbrush.

The sound of a jar lid being unscrewed made me open my eyes.

The gnome had already devoured the cake and drunk the ale. Now, his stubby little fingers were scooping out cheese dip and thrusting it into his mouth.

"Hello," I said.

"What do you want with me?" He was a little smaller than the average plastic garden gnome and not as chubby or cartoonish. His ears were pointy, and his eyes had a faint yellow glow.

"Did you put a curse on a werewolf who was hunting in these woods?"

"What's it to you?" His voice was high-pitched and nasal, as you'd expect of a gnome.

"He's a friend of mine. And a patient. I'm a part-time nurse."

"Along with being a witch?"

"Yes. I also run an occult store. If you need anything, I'll give you twenty percent off. Or, if you need any healthcare, I specialize in supernatural and mythical creatures."

"I don't need anything except to be left alone in my territory."

"Technically, this is a state forest open to the public. Including werewolves."

"I've staked my claim on a particular clearing in these woods. It's where my hoard is buried."

"Hoard of what?"

"That's none of your business. And if I ever catch you there with a metal detector, I'll curse you, too."

"Surely, my werewolf friend wasn't trying to dig up your hoard."

"No. He was lifting his leg and marking his territory on my oak tree. On more than one occasion. How disgusting! I punished him like he deserved."

"Your punishment was excessive. Harry is a husband,

grandfather, and president of his HOA. He needs to return to his human state."

"That's his problem."

"Will you please consider lifting your curse?" I worried that I might have to fight the gnome.

"What's in it for me?"

"A solemn promise that he will never again enter your clearing and pee on your oak tree."

"That's not enough."

"What more do you want from us?"

The gnome grinned evilly. "Cheese dip. Whenever he enters this forest, he must bring cheese dip. And not the spicy nacho kind. No *queso*. I want the regular, bland, processed cheese dip. Like this." He held up the now-empty jar.

"Um, okay. No problem."

"And a can of ale to chase it down. English ale."

"Harry can do that. So, is this a deal? Will you lift your curse?"

"I will. Bring the werewolf here."

I didn't want to allow the gnome out of my sight because I didn't trust that he'd stay. I called Cynthia and asked her to bring Harry here, giving her rough directions.

Soon, an approaching flashlight probed the trees.

"Tell them to turn off that light," the gnome demanded.

I relayed the message to Cynthia, and the light went out.

Feet and paws shuffled on the trail nearby.

"We're just off the trail to your right beside a flat rock," I said.

Harry appeared with Cynthia behind him. When he saw the gnome, he crouched in a submissive position and whined.

"You nasty beast," the gnome said, oblivious to the fact that this beast could bite him in half without effort. "I agree to lift your curse under certain conditions."

I conveyed the instructions Harry must follow if he entered this forest again.

"Isn't that cheese dip bad for you?" Cynthia asked.

"It doesn't matter," I said. "Does Harry agree to bring those items and to stop marking the tree in the gnome's clearing?"

Harry let out a brief howl.

"That was a very enthusiastic yes," Cynthia said.

The gnome walked over to Harry, again without the slightest sign of fear. He pointed at the wolf with both hands, muttered something in his gnomish tongue, then waved his arms in a circular motion.

Harry got out of his submissive crouch and let out a yip of joy. He immediately began to shift.

Shifting is somewhat painful, and I hated to watch it, but I couldn't tear my eyes away. The light from the quarter moon was faint, but Harry was visible as he contorted and twitched, his body reconfiguring to accommodate a human skeleton, his muzzle retreating into his face, fingers growing from his paws. The wolf hair fell off in clumps onto the forest floor.

Harry, the human, was back, crawling on all fours as he regained his bearings. He was naked, flabby, and covered with tattoos—the Harry we loved and missed.

I looked toward the rock to find the gnome had disappeared. All my offerings to him were gone, except for the empty can of ale and jar of cheese dip.

I handed Harry my tote bag so he could cover himself below the waist.

"Did you learn your lesson?" I asked. "Werewolves aren't apex predators when they trespass into the territory of a magical creature."

"I learned, all right."

"Will you ever return to this forest?"

"You bet. There are tons of critters here to hunt. A nice possum midnight snack is easily worth the cheese dip and ale."

When I returned home, I slept well, satisfied that my magic had helped someone's life for the better.

CHAPTER 21
HIDDEN SECRETS

Matt called me the next day. I could tell instantly from his tone of voice that he had bad news.

"I've talked to several of Igor's scam slaves about their experiences there," he said. "But I also wanted extra confirmation that Igor was the murderer."

I had a bad feeling about where this was going.

"On the night that Mr. Bokor was murdered, and the morning of Brad's murder, Igor had alibis. The workers who were on duty during the times of death claim that Igor was there at the office."

"Come on, they were mesmerized," I said. "Their memories have no legitimacy at all. You should have seen what you were like when you were mesmerized. You didn't even hear me when I spoke to you."

"Well, Igor was their boss. They would hear him."

"He could have easily mesmerized them to believe he was in the garage workspace when he actually wasn't."

"To cover that possibility, I spoke to another witness."

"Who?"

"I stopped by Igor's house during the day and spoke to his human housekeeper. Funny, but she looks like you."

I ignored his editorial comment. "What did she say?"

"Igor was kind of agoraphobic. He rarely left the house. As you know, he preyed upon delivery drivers and probably his scam slaves. The housekeeper lives at the house and said she remembers he was at home when the murders occurred. In fact, the only time he has left in recent weeks was the evening when he abducted us."

"But he had a motive to kill them: all the money of his that was squandered. Plus, he sounded angry that Mr. Bokor hadn't produced a hybrid who could work as a scammer."

"I would agree, except for his alibis."

"The housekeeper was lying."

"Believe what you want. I believe the killer is still out there."

I was silent as I stewed.

"Come on, Missy. I know how important justice is to you. How can you live with yourself when there's the slightest chance that you're wrong about Igor, and the murderer walks away free?"

"You don't have to lay it on so thick."

"You never finished searching Mr. Bokor's house for secret compartments. Igor interrupted us."

I sighed. "Okay, I'll go back there. But even if I find a secret compartment, there's no guarantee it's holding something useful to us."

"There's only one way to find out."

I sighed again.

MY EMOTION-SENSING CLOUD was activated as I strolled through Mr. Bokor's house again. I was surprised my own negative emotions about being here didn't light up the cloud. Each visit here had led to unexpected and unpleasant encounters. Matt appeared to be just as nervous as I was.

We didn't talk, though. I couldn't be distracted while maintaining the spell. My natural sensitivity to others' emotions helped power the spell. That, and the power charm clutched in my left hand.

I visited the other bedrooms I hadn't entered before, but found them both empty of furniture and any trace of human energy. Why had Mr. Bokor purchased such a gigantic house when he didn't need all this space?

I checked the kitchen again. There were plenty of emotions present, all overpowered by the fear we experienced here the other night. I sensed nothing consistent with furtiveness.

After touring every room and bathroom, including the garage, I was about to give up. Florida homes don't have basements, at least not in South Florida, because the underground water table is too close to the surface. All that remained to be searched were closets in the common areas and the laundry room.

Of course, in a home like this, the laundry room had to be extravagant. Aside from the high-end appliances, there was a large sink, built-in drying racks, storage cabinets, and a large counter for folding.

A cabinet beneath the counter was drawing my attention. As I knelt to look inside, the cloud around my head lit up like a winning slot machine.

The cabinet was empty, no surprise. I reached to the rear and ran my fingers along the back panel. Sure enough, I felt a seam or crack. Following it, I could tell it was a rectangle about the size of a book. Using my fingernails, I pried out the cabinet panel.

Behind it was a hole cut into the drywall. Shining my phone's flashlight into the opening, I saw what appeared to be a large postcard.

I plucked it out and immediately recognized it.

It was the same invitation my mother had sent to me, threatening death if the recipient didn't join the coven. As someone who also practiced black magic, Mr. Bokor was much more of a rival and threat to my mother than I was.

I guessed he never RSVP'd.

Why hadn't I suspected my mother earlier?

"YOUR THEORY MAKES all sorts of sense," Matt said after I showed him the invitation. "But it doesn't explain why the realtor was murdered."

"Like you said when we suspected Trevor, maybe my mother or her lackeys went to the suites to search Mr. Bokor's office, and Brad confronted them."

"Yeah. I can see why they'd want to search his office. There might be valuable spell books and powerful tools of magic in there."

"So, what do we do?" I asked with a whine. "I've dreaded so much having another confrontation with her."

"Let's try to gather more evidence before you confront anyone."

"Right. Hmm, I wonder if any other witches or sorcerers have turned up dead."

"Not in Jellyfish Beach. Murders are so rare here. Prior to these recent killings, we hadn't had any since the cases involving the ogres."

"Mother's coven covers several counties because there aren't many practitioners of magic in this part of Florida. Can you check the newspaper's records for other similar murders in the region? Ideally, unsolved ones, but mother and her lackeys could have killed someone, and an innocent person was blamed."

"You're casting too wide a net," Matt said, trying to rub the tension from his face. "Is there a list of witches?"

"No. Only the one that Mother has put together. We can narrow down the murders by looking for similar means of death. Both Mr. Bokor and Brad were killed with an ice pick-like weapon. It could be a ceremonial one."

"Wounds like that are unusual enough to stand out. I'll look into it."

In the meantime, I would check with the small number of witches I knew to see if they received the threatening invitation to join Mother's coven. Harriet had already joined. Angela, who had reached the advanced level of mage, was the most powerful magic-maker I knew, aside from my mother. The more casual witches in the area might escape Mother's notice, but not Angela. I called and invited her to coffee the next day.

When Angela arrived at the 1890s-era home downtown that was now a coffee shop, she couldn't hide that she was still peeved at me.

I stood and gave the elderly librarian a peck on the cheek.

"I apologize, again, for thinking for one second that the Society had Mr. Bokor killed," I said. "Igor Stanisloopsky was so adamant about it."

"I can't say I'm sad to learn he was destroyed," she said, sitting down at my corner table. "We received too many reports of him preying upon delivery drivers. If only more vampires would get their meals from the Blood Bus."

The bus, which traveled to shopping centers and other public places, took blood donations from unsuspecting altruists. Instead of sending the donations to blood banks, the truck delivered them each night to vampires, such as many of the residents of Squid Tower.

"Yeah, some vampires prefer to hunt because of their predatory instincts, but Igor didn't even hunt. He simply ambushed his victims at his front door."

After Angela's coffee and my tea arrived, she glanced at her watch.

"How can I help you?" She was all business with me.

I hoped I could repair our friendship and continue my magic lessons with her soon.

"I wonder if my mother ordered the murder of Mr. Bokor because he didn't join her coven. Did you receive an invitation to join?"

"I did. And I threw it away. Though it kept flying out of my recycling bin. I ended up burning it in my fireplace."

"I received one, too. I can't bring myself to dismiss it as easily as you."

"I'm a mage. I'm not afraid of your mother's sloppy black magic. And it's unlikely her thugs can get me with an ice pick."

"Speaking of which, have you heard of any ceremonial weapons that make wounds like that?"

"A rondel."

"A what?"

"A medieval dagger with a round handle and a needle-like blade," she explained. "It was made for penetrating the armor of a fallen knight."

"The Knights Simplar might have one of those."

Angela nodded while she sipped her coffee.

"You don't seem concerned," I said.

"I already told you I wasn't."

"What about other witches in the area? Have you heard of anyone else receiving these threats?"

"One witch I know said she had."

"Shouldn't we do something about this?"

Angela put her coffee down and leaned back. "Look, my primary duty to the supernatural community is to serve the Friends of Cryptids Society. My job isn't to police the magic practitioners."

"What if someone else gets murdered?"

"I don't know what you want me to do."

"Stop my mother and her cult-like followers."

She shook her head sadly. "You just don't get it."

"I guess not. What do you mean?"

"We can't start a war. It would expose the supernatural community. Think of all the inconvenient questions our battle with Lord Arseton and the demon in the laundromat caused."

"True." The police had interrogated me about the damage to the facility.

"If the murderer was human, the only way to handle this is through law enforcement. You need to find evidence that someone from your mother's coven was involved. I will not use my magic to blow up stuff based on nothing but suspicion."

Great. She wanted me to do actual, painstaking investigating? That's no fun.

Despite my disappointment in not having a magic-wielding ally to help me wage war against my mother, we spent the rest of our time together making pleasant small talk. Hopefully, it healed some of the ill will I had caused when accusing the Society and, indirectly, her in the murder of Mr. Bokor.

Angela stood up. "This has been delightful, but I'm due to meet a friend now."

"The coffee's on me, of course," I said.

"Thank you." She gave me a grandmotherly kiss on the cheek. "Let me know of any developments."

She went outside, and I watched her through the home's large bay window. An attractive woman, likely in her fifties, waited for her on the sidewalk. Before they walked away together, Angela kissed her deeply—and there was nothing grandmotherly about it.

There was a lot more to Angela than I knew or guessed at.

I HAD the rest of the day off, so I decided to begin the painstaking investigating. When I was released from Mother's apartment after the Knights Simplar had abducted me, they hadn't put the hood back on my head and driven me home. They'd simply let me go. I guess being the daughter of a saint comes with benefits.

Therefore, I knew exactly where her apartment was. The most tedious, painstaking kind of investigating was to do what they did in the cop shows: stake out her apartment building. Sit for hours in my car and hope no one notices me.

The building was two blocks away from the main street. The ornate white building looked like it had been built in the 1920s. I parked across the street, in front of a nail salon, where I could see whoever left and entered through the front door.

Okay. I'm doing a stakeout. I'm reconnoitering. I've got this place under surveillance.

The clock on my dashboard said I'd been here for three minutes. And I was bored with it already.

Being in South Florida, I had to keep the engine running so I wouldn't die from lack of air conditioning. I unwisely didn't fill the tank before embarking on this mission, and I wondered how long the engine would run before I needed to head to the gas station. That would be the exact moment someone important entered or exited the building.

My stomach growled. I should have brought snacks with me.

I wondered, who would someone important be? How

would seeing this someone give me a eureka moment that would prove the coven was behind the murders?

I had no idea. But this was what cops did—sit in their cars on stakeouts.

And sit with a growling stomach. The aroma of garlic and olive oil wafted through my car's air filters from the Italian restaurant at the corner. My stomach roared at the indignity.

Wait—the door of the apartment building opened! An old man with a walker tottered out. I bet this was the clueless guy who rode the elevator with us while I was being abducted. He was *not* defined as someone important.

Nothing happened for the longest time. I turned on the radio to entertain myself. I had the first hint that I needed to pee.

The clock on the dashboard said I'd been on my stakeout for all of eighteen minutes.

Movement caught my eye. A shirtless, overweight man rode an electric scooter past the building. I couldn't tear my eyes from the sight, like staring at a horrible car wreck. Scantily clad people who shouldn't be scantily clad were much too common in Florida. Yet I couldn't help but watch him and wonder why.

By focusing on him, I almost missed her leaving the building. It took me a moment to recognize her because it was so unexpected to see her here.

Eva, the receptionist from the executive suites, reached the sidewalk and walked quickly down the block. She wore sunglasses and a small backpack.

I would classify her as someone important.

She turned the corner at the end of the block, and I put the car into gear, moving slowly so I wouldn't catch up with her.

There was virtually no traffic on this street, so that wasn't a problem.

I turned the corner. My guess was she was headed for the small municipal parking garage up ahead. Sure enough, she turned into it and disappeared into the stairwell.

Time to park and continue my stakeout.

CHAPTER 22

SHE'S HARDLY A SAINT

A Mercedes sedan came down the garage ramp. I figured it was Eva but wasn't certain because of her window tinting. But when she turned onto the street and drove right by me, I got a better look. It was Eva.

Thanks to the light traffic, I could follow her with lots of space between us. I didn't worry about her seeing my car behind her. She wouldn't recognize it. It didn't look like an unmarked police car; nor did it look like a witch's car. It was the kind of car you looked away from because you felt sorry for whomever was driving it.

Why hadn't I dipped into the money I received from the Friends of Cryptids Society? Most of it went into keeping the botanica afloat. The rest went into a retirement account that had lain fallow ever since I drained it after I quit my job at the hospital and worked as a home-health nurse for monsters, when I didn't think I'd survive long enough to retire.

Eva drove south of downtown to a section with lots of new

condos and townhomes. She pulled into the fanciest townhome development in the area. The parking lot was behind the homes that lined the street.

It occurred to me that my plans for a stakeout didn't go any further than the staking out part. Sure, now I knew where she lived, but that didn't tell me much.

Was Eva leaving Mother's apartment building because she had business with Mother? Or was she just visiting another tenant? Was she a member of the coven? What did that mean, given that the two murder victims worked in the same office suites as she?

I parked in a visitor's spot near Eva's space. When she got out of her car, I could think of nothing to do other than confront her.

"Hi, Eva!" I called. "Do you live here?"

She frowned because it was a stupid question, she didn't want to see me, or both.

"Yes. Were you following me?"

"I saw you leaving an apartment building on Periwinkle Avenue. My mother lives there. I was wondering if you knew her."

"Your mother? What's her name?"

"She goes by the name of Ruth Bent."

She gasped. "Saint Ruth?"

"She's hardly a saint. Believe me."

She didn't take offense at what I said, like Lord Arseton would have.

"Are you a member of her coven?" I asked.

Eva looked around, afraid of someone eavesdropping.

"Come inside." She beckoned for me to follow her.

We walked to a nearby townhome, and she unlocked the door. We went only as far as the high-end kitchen. Her body language made it clear she didn't want me to proceed any farther into her home.

"I had no choice," she said grimly. "I was forced to join."

"I didn't realize you're a witch. Don't worry, I sympathize with you. I received an invitation to join the coven, threatening my life if I didn't. I assume you did, too?"

"Yes." She was opening up to me more. "I didn't know you were a witch, too."

I nodded.

"I guess I'm not really a witch or a bruja," she said. "I was fascinated by Jules' voodoo sorcery, and he taught me a little. You could say I was his acolyte. I wish I knew how Saint Ruth found out about me."

"Through her black magic. And the demons she enlists to help her."

"Demons?"

"Yeah. You're obviously new to the cult."

"You call it a cult?"

"Yes. It's more of a cult than a coven, all centered on one malignant narcissist."

"They're scary. I didn't want to join, but I feared for my life."

I paused before my next question, wanting to ask it just right.

"Did they kill Mr. Bokor?"

Eva's eyes widened in fear. "I think so."

"You *think* so?"

"Yes, um, someone was talking about a sorcerer who

wouldn't submit to them," she blurted out. "That they had taken care of him."

"What about Brad? Did they kill him, too? He wasn't a witch, was he?"

"No, Brad would never understand magic. I guess they killed him because he was in early that morning and surprised them when they wanted to break into Jules' office."

It was the same theory Matt and I had.

"When you met with the coven, did you see any dorky guys who pretended to be medieval knights?"

"Yeah, there was one guy who dressed like he was part of a Renaissance festival. And during the ceremony, he wore a monk's habit with a cowl over his head."

"Did he wear in his belt a dagger with a round handle and a long, needle-like blade?"

"I don't know. Wait, yes. Yes, he did."

"Are you sure?"

"Uh-huh. It was scary-looking." She looked at the clock on the wall. "So, like, I have to get to the office. I told my manager I had a doctor's appointment. Why would the coven hold a meeting on a weekday morning?"

"My mother's whims are your commands. Thank you for your time. I might be in touch again."

I wanted to tell her I might mention her name as a witness when I went to the police, but I realized that would scare her away.

During my drive home, I analyzed my interaction with Eva. Her being a member of the coven was shocking, but I totally bought the explanation that she learned magic from Mr. Bokor. She didn't come from a nationality that believed in voodoo, but working in those office suites would put voodoo in your face on a daily basis. Mr. Bokor hadn't hid what he did; in fact, he'd flaunted it. The clouds of incense escaping his office and his chimera pet made his activities even more pronounced.

What nagged at my mind was the incongruity of Eva's young age and junior job title with her conspicuous wealth. Driving a luxury car and living in that fancy townhome didn't fit. She must come from money. I hoped she hadn't gotten the money from Mr. Bokor in some unsavory arrangement.

As soon as I got home, I went to my computer and visited the property appraiser's site, curious to see how much Eva's townhome was worth. Even if she was only renting it, I could look it up by the address.

When I did, my mouth dropped open. Not only because of the high appraisal of the home.

But because it was owned by Brad Keeble.

This was the property Matt had speculated was an income property. Renting it to a coworker wasn't a crime. But it was interesting that Brad's wife's name was not on the deed, while it was occupied by an attractive, young, unmarried woman.

Get your mind out of the gutter, Missy!

Still, I was left with the uneasy feeling that much of what Eva had told me today was a pile of baloney. As a witch, I had a lot of empathy and was super-sensitive to emotional energy. I just knew Eva wasn't being completely honest with me.

But I couldn't tell which things she told me were falsehoods or if there were lies of omission.

I called Matt and filled him in.

"That is crazy," he said. "We need to take a closer look at Eva."

"I watched you get some pretty close and intimate looks at her."

"Now, now, you know that's not true. She's pretty, but too young for me."

"Since when has a man been turned off by a woman being too young?"

"More often than you apparently realize."

The rattling of keyboard strokes came through the phone.

"I'm looking up Brad again in public records. Here's a notice his condo is now under foreclosure."

"I guess because he lost all his money to Mr. Bokor. That means Eva won't have a place to live. Desperate people do desperate things."

"You should have used your truth spell on her."

"I didn't think there was a need to. I still don't know. It's odd discovering she has a secret life dabbling in voodoo and joined Mother's coven. I don't blame her for joining it, though. Most people don't take death threats very well."

"So, Eva was involved in Mr. Bokor's sorcery," Matt said. "She might have been romantically involved with Brad. At the very least, she was his tenant. Could she have been an investor in the real estate deal as well? I still haven't found the names of the partners of the shell company."

Suddenly, a minor fragment of memory came to the forefront. It was about a floor plan of the executive suites we'd found in Mr. Bokor's office when we first searched it.

It had seemed irrelevant: a layout of the different offices, with Mr. Bokor's highlighted with a yellow marker. They probably gave it to him when he signed the lease.

What made me remember it was the fact that he'd written on it. He hadn't penciled in the names of the other people in their offices they occupied, as you'd expect. Rather, two or three offices had numbers written in their spaces. Large numbers with zeros and commas. What did the numbers represent? They didn't appear to be dimensions. What if they were dollars?

And if I remembered correctly, a number was written beside the rectangle that represented the receptionist's desk.

"We need to return to the executive suites for another search," I said. "Pick me up, and I'll explain on our way there."

"I hope the alarm system doesn't keep a record of your constantly disarming it."

"Frankly, I don't care."

When we arrived at the office building in Matt's truck, I began preparing my unlocking spell. Fortunately, I had the foresight last time we were here to write down the alarm code. But when we got off the elevator at the executive suites, a wrench was thrown in the gears.

The lights were on in the suites. The cleaning service was in there.

"I guess we'll have to wait," Matt said.

"Nonsense. I don't have the patience for that."

Floor-to-ceiling windows faced the receptionist's desk and the facility's logo on the wall behind it. I moved to an angle that allowed a view down the hallway to my left. I saw a man with a trash barrel on wheels go into one of the offices.

I felt a little guilty putting a spell on an innocent bystander, but it was a completely harmless spell, and my guilt didn't stop me.

When the man exited the office, I cast a sleep spell. He immediately sat on the floor, leaned back against the wall, and went to dreamland.

He'd left the main door unlocked, so I didn't have to cast a spell for that. We went inside, past the sleeping man, straight for Mr. Bokor's office. It was unlocked, too.

Going by memory, I opened the shallow drawer in the middle of the desk. The floor plan was still there. I laid it on top of the desk and studied it.

In the space that represented Brad's office was a number written in pencil: 1,575,000. Two offices away—I think it was the attorney's—a number had been written and erased. And yes, beside Eva's desk was a number larger than Brad's.

I knew now in my gut that these numbers were the dollar amounts invested in the failed development project.

"Look at this," I said to Matt. "These are Mr. Bokor's investors who got shafted. Brad and Eva."

"Well, well. She was involved in everything. But she's only in her twenties. How did she get all that cash?"

"I don't know. But think about it. She's living in a condo that Brad owned. Was he renting it to her because he knew her, or was she living there for free because they had something going on?"

"My thoughts exactly."

"And she admitted she was Mr. Bokor's acolyte. That would explain why he invited her into the development deal."

"I see where you're going, and I don't like it."

I marched up the hall to Eva's desk. "This is where we need to be searching."

I pulled open the drawers of her desk, not quite sure what I was searching for. Would she keep a blood-stained rondel dagger in here? Unlikely.

Behind her desk, around the partial wall that bore the executive suites' logo, was a supply closet. I yanked open the doors and looked at boxes of copier paper and envelopes. Never underestimate the damage a paper cut can do.

On the bottom shelf was a brown plastic box, shaped like a book. I snapped open the clasp and opened it to find an office tool kit. Inside were screwdrivers, pliers, an adjustable wrench, a socket wrench, and a tiny hammer suitable for driving picture hooks into drywall.

There was an assortment of screwdrivers in different sizes, flat-head and Phillips-head.

One flat-head and one Phillips-head were missing.

"What do you think of that?" I asked.

"Are you implying she killed two men with screwdrivers?"

"People have been killed with more unlikely weapons. The Phillips-head caused the puncture wounds. The flat-head did the slashing."

"Let's call Shortle and tell her what we found."

"I really think we're on to something with Eva," I said. "I

feel it in my gut. But this isn't enough evidence in the eyes of law enforcement."

"We should still tell Shortle."

"We will, but we need to get more. Like a confession."

"You mean using your truth spell?"

"Yes. And you'll shoot video with your phone of what she says."

As we left the office, I broke the sleep spell on the cleaning guy. We were already on the elevator before he was awake enough to see us. We got into Matt's truck, and he turned to me with a worried expression.

"You realize that even if she's home, she could simply refuse to answer the door. Or even call the police on us."

"I doubt she'll want anything to do with the police. And if she doesn't let us in, I'll ambush her another time."

During the drive, I called Shortle. How many witches have a detective's private number? Not many, I would suspect.

She didn't answer. Okay, just because I had her number, it didn't mean she wanted to take random calls from a witch. I left a long message with information about the murders, reciting the suspicions I had and the evidence we'd found, which were circumstantial. I added I was going to have another chat with Eva. Maybe that would light a fire under Shortle's butt.

When we pulled into the townhome complex, I was relieved to see Eva's car in its place and lights on in her home. We parked and sat in the truck, trying to work up our courage.

"I think the angle we'll take at the beginning with her is that we're going after the coven," I said. "If she's the murderer

—and that's a big if—we don't know if she did it under orders of my mother or for her own reasons. I suspect it's the latter."

"Me, too."

"She joined the coven under duress, and I bet she'll be happy to pin the murders on them. That is unless the truth spell reveals something else. Are you ready to go in?"

He swallowed nervously. "Yeah."

CHAPTER 23
IN DEEP VOODOO DOO-DOO

We walked to Eva's door, and I rang the bell. I sensed we were being studied by the doorbell camera. Fortunately, she knew both of us.

The door opened a crack.

"Yes?" She wore a T-shirt and sweatpants. Her eyes looked sleepy.

"Sorry to bother you so late," I said with a fake smile. "I had a few more questions. Matt is investigating the coven, and I really think they're behind the murders."

"Oh, I can't talk about the coven publicly. They'd kill me."

"This is off the record," Matt said. "Your name won't appear in anything I write. I just need background information." He gave his cutest grin. "I swear you'll be safe."

The grin seemed to work. "Okay, I'll talk to you for a little while, but I need to go to bed soon."

"This will be brief," he promised.

She opened the door for us and led the way to the dining

room, where we sat at a table that was too big for the space. Her home had luxury finishes and expensive furniture, but didn't truly feel lived in, in the same way Mr. Bokor's home felt.

"Your home is beautiful," I said.

"Thank you. My parents passed away two years ago and left me some money." It was as if she knew we wondered how she afforded the place.

"I'm so sorry," I said.

Matt mumbled his condolences.

"Let's get right into it so that we don't waste your time," he said. "The coven has been on our radar for a while because of several incidents of vandalism at houses of worship and an attack on a charity fundraising event."

"That's horrible. Why would they do that?"

"They're deranged," I said. "They need to be stopped."

She nodded in agreement.

Matt asked her questions about the threatening invitation she had received, and I used the opportunity to cast my truth spell. Carefully, with as little movement as possible, I removed the pouch of powder from my pocket and sprinkled some on Eva's feet beneath the table.

Within seconds, her eyes became glassy, and her face animated, as if she were on amphetamines. The urge to unburden herself was clear in her expression.

Matt looked at me, and I gave him a slight nod. I would take over the interview now.

I began with simple questions to dispel any resistance she had that would fight the spell.

"Is it true that Brad owns this property?"

"Yes. I've been renting from him. I was thinking about buying the place before..." She fought back tears.

"Will you buy it now from his heirs?"

She shook her head sadly. "No."

"Because Brad's wife doesn't like you?"

"That horrible woman hates me, but Brad was going to leave her. He loved me. Or so I thought."

"You had a relationship with him?"

She nodded, and her eyes filled with tears.

"If his wife puts the townhome on the market, would you buy it from her anonymously?"

"No."

"Is it because you can't afford it?"

She nodded.

"Did you lose money recently on a failed investment deal?"

"It didn't fail!" she said angrily. "It died because Jules pulled the plug. Because he took all our money and blew it on, I don't know what."

"Why were you investing with him in the first place? Didn't it seem risky?"

"Brad talked me into it. Jules made a lot of money flipping homes and had a magic touch with real estate. Jules said he would ordinarily not take money from someone inexperienced like me, but he trusted me because I was his acolyte. I helped him with his sorcery. But he and Brad betrayed me."

"How so?"

"After they took my money, they said my share of the property would be much smaller than they had promised. When I complained, Brad said they were giving me my money back and cutting me out of the deal. But they never paid me a cent. Brad broke up with me and said I had to move out of this place. Jules said he didn't want me to assist him anymore. They both gave me the cold shoulder."

"That must have been horrible, especially when sharing the same workplace."

"Yes! I was so miserable, but I couldn't afford to quit my job. Then, Jules pulled the plug on the entire project. That meant Brad lost all his money, too. Plus, he was deeply in debt."

"Did that make you feel any better?"

"Not really."

"Did Brad kill Mr. Bokor?"

She shook her head.

"Did you?"

Eva stared at the table without answering, but I felt her many emotions building in intensity, about to boil over.

"Eva?"

She turned her face to me. Her lips quivered, and her fists clenched. She wanted so badly to unload her anger, but a small part of her knew better and was resisting.

I fed more energy to the truth spell, and it pushed her over the edge.

"A stupid drunk driver took my parents from me, and I just wanted to make the money they left me grow. I wanted to live comfortably after so much was taken from me. But these snakes took my money, too! The snakes thought I was a stupid kid and took all my money. They took everything from me! Everything!"

I didn't make a sound while she was unburdening herself. Matt surreptitiously filmed her with his phone's camera.

"Then I got this letter that threatened me if I didn't join the coven! They threatened to kill me just because I was helping Jules with his sorcery. And he wouldn't even speak to me and tell me what I should do about it. The stupid, greedy snake! One day, after everyone had gone home, Brad was yelling at him about the money, and Jules walked by my desk on his way out. He gave me this arrogant smirk. And something in me snapped."

Eva stopped, seeming to relive that moment. I waited. Please, please go on.

"It was time for him to get what he deserved. I looked around for something I could use as a weapon. All I found were screwdrivers. I followed his car. When he left the botanica, I confronted him in the parking lot. He had this dismissive attitude. That smirk. I lost it. I barely remember what I did."

"How did he get into the dumpster?" I asked carefully.

"He climbed in to get away from me. Then I went home, cleaned up. I put the incident behind me. I walled it off in a box and erased the memory. But not long after, I was in the office early, and Brad came in. All I wanted was a little understanding from him. After all, he got stiffed by Jules, too. I just wanted a little sympathy for all I had lost. We used to be lovers, and I put my hate for him aside and just wanted to talk.

"But he told me to get out of his office," she continued. "And the rage came back. I had cleaned the screwdrivers and put them back in the case, but somehow, they ended up in my hands again. I don't even remember killing Brad, only the moments right after. This time, I threw away the screwdrivers."

She was silent for a while. I wondered if the spell was still working.

But Eva noticed the top of Matt's phone poking up above the edge of the table with its lenses aiming at her.

"Are you making a video of this?" she asked in a voice hoarse from her shouting.

By the look in her eyes, the truth spell had worn off prematurely. And she was beyond angry.

Then, as the expression goes, or as my adoptive parents would put it, all heck broke loose.

Invisible ropes bound me to my chair, and Matt toppled backward from his.

Eva got to her feet and pointed her finger at him.

"You will be the horse for the loa who comes to this world to ride you to death."

I didn't know much about voodoo, but loas are spirits or gods that serve as intermediaries between humans and the divine creator. In voodoo ceremonies, the person possessed by a spirit was called the horse. How he behaved would depend on which loa took over his body and how benevolent or evil it was.

Matt jumped to his feet and began dancing, his arms held parallel to the floor, his body spasming, his head twitching, his eyes rolled back in his head. He wouldn't win a dance contest, but he was scaring me to death.

"And you," she pointed her finger at me, "will stay in your chair while I smash his phone to pieces."

Of course, I had been building a protection spell the moment she lost her cool. When the force of her magic had seized me, my chair almost tipped over backward. I was still in command of my body, though, aside from the invisible ropes.

"You're more than an acolyte," I said. "Don't sell yourself short. You know quite a lot of magic."

"Shut up! You tricked me into saying that stuff. It's all untrue. I made it all up."

"Right. But I'm serious—you're good at this."

"What does it matter? Jules could barely make a living at it. He had to rip off that rich vampire to afford nice things. And now, I have nothing."

I needed to get Matt's phone before she did, but whatever spell she had cast on me kept me bound to the chair.

I had my telekinesis, though. Focusing on the phone, which Matt had dropped on the floor when he started dancing, I sent it sliding beneath a large armoire against the wall.

Eva cursed and got down on her hands and knees to reach for the phone.

I'd never before heard of a battle between voodoo and elemental magic. In Eva's hands, voodoo was much stronger than I had realized.

Still, she was besting me only physically. My mind was still free. My energies were still strong and available for harvesting, as I cast an immobility spell upon her.

It would have worked, I'm certain. If Matt hadn't danced over and knocked me and my chair over.

The loa that possessed him was a big problem. There are said to be thousands of loas, many of which humans don't even know about. And the one possessing Matt was obviously a powerful one.

Matt loomed over me as I lay sideways on the floor, tied by

magic to my chair. His face contorted as he struggled against the spirit that possessed him.

"Kill her, Kalfu!" Eva shouted.

I didn't know a human could give loas commands, but Kalfu heard her.

Matt bent over me and grabbed my neck with both hands. He shouldn't have been able to penetrate my protection spell. Either it had failed, or the loa broke through it.

"No, Matt, no! It's me, Missy. Don't hurt me."

He hesitated. His eyes became normal, and, for the briefest moment, I saw Matt looking back at me. But then his eyes rolled back until only the whites were showing.

And his grip tightened. Matt fought the spirit, and his hands loosened slightly.

Now was not the time to do any deep thinking, but I had no choice. Before Matt's grip cut off my air, I needed to scour my memories of the loa figurines in the botanica and the random facts I'd learned from Madame Tibodet.

From what I recalled, Kalfu was the evil loa of the spirits of the night and was represented by a tall, powerful man.

If my memory was correct, his enemy was Legba, the benevolent loa of the spirits of the day. We had a ceramic figurine of him in the botanica. I remembered it because it was on the shelf below the figurine of St. Francis who had an annoying habit of animating and speaking to me, pestering me for being a lapsed Catholic.

Normally, my magic had nothing to do with the stage magic you're familiar with, in which an entertainer performs sleight-of-hand tricks and misdirection. But I did know how to create illusions; I just rarely had a reason to do so.

Tonight, I had an excellent reason.

I created a three-dimensional illusion of Legba. Call it a witch's version of a hologram, if you will. The elderly man stood beside Matt, holding an ax over his head.

"Kalfu," I said. "Papa Legba is here for you."

Matt turned his head and saw the illusion. Or, rather, the spirit that possessed him saw it. He released my neck, growled like an animal, and lunged at the apparition.

Now was my opportunity. I cast my immobility spell again. Just as Eva retrieved Matt's phone from beneath the armoire, she froze like a mannequin.

I cast the same spell at Matt. I felt bad doing it to a friend, but I think I'd be excused, considering the circumstances. Matt stood there, frozen. He was no longer a threat to me, but he was still possessed.

I manipulated my illusion of Legba to swing his ax in Matt's direction. An eerie howl came from Matt's frozen lips, and I sensed a supernatural force sweep past me like a gust of wind.

Matt's eyes became normal again. Just in case, I wanted to free myself before I freed him. I went into deep meditation and used my energies to probe the spell that bound me to the chair. It was constructed differently than the elemental-magic spells I use, but the fundamental energy it was based upon was similar.

In my mind I conjured an image of the invisible ropes around me and used my negation spell to sever the strands one by one until they fell apart and dissolved.

My back ached as I got to my feet and approached Matt. I peered into his eyes. The only parts of him that could move were his heart, lungs, and other essential body parts. No voluntary movements were possible. His eyelids blinked, revealing eyes that were lucid and normal. I broke the immobility spell.

"What the heck happened to me?" he asked.

"I'll explain later. Get your phone from Eva. You won't believe how close she came to deleting the confessional video you shot of her."

I looked down at her as she sat frozen on the floor. The murderer and budding voodoo sorceress stared at me with angry eyes. She had almost killed me, but I still felt a small bit of sympathy for her and all her losses.

The doorbell rang.

Matt and I looked at each other, startled.

"Maybe she'd ordered a pizza," he said.

I opened the door to find Detective Shortle.

"What are you doing here?" she asked.

"I have the same question for you."

"I got your message and came here to speak to Ms. Martin."

"You need to arrest her. After you see our video, you'll agree. And if you don't mind my asking, why the heck did it take you so long to get here?"

CHAPTER 24
DEADLINE

After a long day at the botanica, then dropping off a bottle of iron supplements to a vampire former patient, I returned home to a rude surprise. The smell of cigarette smoke.

The source could be Tony breaking my rule and smoking inside the garage. Or it could be much more disturbing.

I turned on the living room lights to find my mother sitting on the couch, drinking a beer, stubbing out a cigarette in an ornamental dish I kept on my coffee table.

"How did you get in here?" I asked.

"You know how. And my spells open locks and defeat magical wards faster than yours do."

"What do you want?"

"I heard you had one of my young coven members arrested."

"I didn't *have her arrested*. I found evidence that she was a murderer."

She cackled and broke into coughing.

"You're such a do-gooder. It's pathetic. That young woman did us a favor by killing the voodoo sorcerer. We would have had to kill him eventually because he wouldn't join my coven and his money ran out."

"His money?" I asked. "What are you talking about? He was paying you?"

She cackled again, but managed to not cough.

"That idiot was flashing his money around, with his huge homes and boats and such. Voodoo bokors never get *that* rich. That's how he got my attention. He was the first magician around here that we went after."

"You were extorting him?"

"Of course! I told him he had to join the coven or die. But if he didn't want to die, he could send cash every week. Lots of cash. And when I learned about his creations—his little hybrids—I threatened to kill them, too. He was quite proud of them."

"That sounds like something you would do."

"Yes, dearie, you know me well. It turns out I was very clever."

"What do you mean?"

"Mr. Bokor had more cash than I ever imagined. Millions. I think he was scamming a group of investors. Little did they know they were investing in me!"

She laughed and fell into a violent cough. I felt no pity for her. In fact, I would shed no tears if she coughed up a lung.

It was reasonable to conclude that Mother was the reason Mr. Bokor ran out of money and the land development venture died. Which led to his and Brad's murders.

The world would be a better place without this woman.

"The stakes are the same for you, dearie, if you don't join the coven," she said. "Just because I brought you into this world doesn't mean I won't usher you out of it."

"If your coven kills anyone, you'll all go to prison. It's that simple."

"The police in this town couldn't find their way out of a paper bag. If we kill someone, it's going to be impossible to trace it to us."

"Don't be so sure of that."

"Missy, the nurse, is now Missy, the detective?"

"I'm just a citizen who doesn't want criminals in my town."

Ruth coughed another laugh. "So naïve. If you don't want anyone to be killed, then you'll have to pay up."

"I told you I don't have much money. It all went into the botanica."

"It would be a shame for your quaint little shop to be driven out of business."

"Did you come here just to threaten me? Because I got your message, and now I need to feed the cats and the iguana."

"What makes you think they're still alive?"

I panicked. Rushing into my bedroom, I turned on the light and looked under the bed. Brenda lay there looking at me with an expression that said, "Get that woman out of this house, and feed me. Now."

Where was Bubba?

I ran out of the room, checked around the cat dishes in the kitchen and the litter box station. Finally, I saw him perched atop a bookcase, watching my mother warily.

But what about Tony? I opened the interior door to the garage. He sat atop my workbench.

“There’s a black-magic sorceress in your house,” he said.

“Yes. I’m well aware.”

I returned to the living room, where Ruth was laughing at me.

“You see, you know they’re vulnerable. You can act all brave if you want when it comes to your own life, but do you want your animals to be killed because of you? Food for thought, dearie.”

She stood and walked to the front door.

“There’s a deadline on the invitation for you to RSVP. Better not miss it.”

She walked out, leaving the door open behind her.

The invitation—or demand—from the coven was still where I had dropped it on an end table in the living room. I didn’t remember a deadline being on there.

I picked it up. I was right. No deadline. Just the red text that had magically appeared warning me that failure to comply would result in death.

But then a straight horizontal line appeared at the bottom of the card. It was red, of course. About an inch long, it extended from the left margin.

As I stared at it, the line grew a fraction of an inch longer. I realized it was like a progress bar on your computer that drives you crazy while you’re waiting for your computer to restart or a website to load. It was, literally, a dead line. If it reaches the right side of the card, I’ll be dead.

Now I know from whom I got my weird sense of humor. Mine, however, was not psychotic.

So much of my work dealing with things that go wrong in the supernatural world requires me to avoid involving the police. But with my mother threatening to kill witches who don't join her coven, I had to warn the police. I called Shortle's private number.

This time, she answered.

"Shortle. How can I help you, Ms. Mindle?"

"I believe the group behind the church defilements is a bunch of people who pretend they're witches," I said, because witchcraft isn't real, right?

"Do you know who they are?"

"I know one is named Ruth Bent. And I've heard they're forcing anyone who claims to be a quote-unquote witch to join the coven under the threat of death if they don't. They haven't killed anyone yet."

"That's good to know."

"But they're capable of it. I wanted to tip you off in case there's a murder."

"Where can I find this Ruth Bent?"

"You can't talk to her about the death threats, or she'll know it was me who told you."

"I want to talk to her about the church vandalism. I need to see evidence of death threats before I accuse her of them."

I gave her the address of the apartment the coven was using. It was better to hold off on giving Shortle my copy of the invitation for now. I was too afraid of my mother.

"By the way," Shortle said, "one of the murder weapons

was found. This is off the record. We haven't announced it to the press, including your boyfriend."

"He's not my boyfriend. Where did you find the screwdriver?"

"In the bottom of a storm drain next to the office building. The city was clearing out debris and found it. A worker had heard about the suspect's arrest and the means of death and notified us. It's a flathead screwdriver that matches the others in the toolset. I figure the Phillips-head is still down in the sewer somewhere."

"Thanks for letting me know. How's the prosecution going?"

"The perp's attorney wants the video confession excluded, of course. We'll see how that goes. How did you get her to open up so much to you?"

"Empathy," I said. "It works like magic."

"I ought to try it. I'm not a very empathetic kind of person."

"No. But you can work on it."

I HAD NOT EXPECTED to see the ad in *The Jellyfish Beach Journal.* It was for a new vegetarian restaurant in town called "The Pasture" that featured "farm-to-fork tapas and other gourmet vegetarian delights for grazing." I had to check it out.

After an excellent dinner, I asked to meet the chef. My server said that wasn't possible, but I asked her to tell him that Missy Mindle would like to say hi. She returned to the table and led me into the kitchen.

Trevor stood behind a prep counter so you could only see him from the waist up. He looked like a typical chef in a baseball cap and white chef's jacket. He smiled when he saw me.

"Congratulations on achieving your dream," I said.

"Thank you. It turns out Igor left me money in his will."

I didn't know how it worked legally when the undead "die." How do you get a death certificate? I hoped I never had to worry about that.

"How's business been?"

"Fantastic. We're already getting a reputation as a hip place to dine."

"Good for you. My meal was wonderful. Do you know how the other hybrids are doing?"

"Even though Igor disliked the Friends of Cryptids Society, he sent them a donation to ensure the best care for Pete. He also donated to the Savanna Safari Park to care for Percy. But Percy still breaks out from time to time. He's too clever and has his magical abilities, as you know. Igor's human housekeeper will care for Jules' monkey-cat, snake, and goats, as well as Igor's cat-dog."

"That's a tall order. What's going to become of the rest of Igor's estate?"

"I heard he has a distant relative overseas he bequeathed it to. The relative is traveling to Florida to decide what to do with the estate."

"Is he or she a vampire?"

"I don't know. But I'm reasonably sure she's not human."

Wonderful, I thought. Yet another monster coming to Jellyfish Beach to keep the Society busy.

I wished Trevor the best and returned home.

I WOKE up early in the morning with a sense of dread. It was only 3:10 a.m., which was much too early for getting up, especially since I had the vampire creative-writing workshop later tonight.

Sleep eluded me, however. So, I got up and made a pot of tea. The cats were thrilled that I was up early because it meant an early breakfast for them. The caffeine from half a cup was enough to make my brain conjure up every half-forgotten detail of things I needed to do.

But I also couldn't stop thinking about the coven's death threat. It was almost as if the invitation was calling me from the living room where I had left it.

I shuffled in my slippers across the hardwood floors into the living room and turned on a lamp. The invitation lay on the end table, appearing the same as when I last saw it. Still, I felt forced to pick it up.

When I touched it, the "deadline" moved at least an inch to the right, now reaching about one-third of the way across the card.

Shortle must have spoken to my mother, who, understandably, was not happy about it. And she knew it must have been me who gave her name to Shortle.

Which meant my death was even more imminent.

CHAPTER 25
SANCTUARY

Mrs. Lupis and Mr. Lopez were once again waiting for me on my front porch. My neighbors, who already thought I was weird, were surely peering through their blinds at my two handlers, wondering what sort of religious evangelists they were. It was getting embarrassing.

"We've come to congratulate you on finding the murderer of the bokor and the realtor," Mr. Lopez said.

"Thank you. I don't understand how you know these things before anyone else does. This wasn't a supernatural crime."

"It had supernatural trimmings," Mrs. Lupis said.

"If you guys are so dialed into the supernatural in this town, can you protect me from my mother's coven? I've been threatened with death if I don't join."

"If it came to that, we wouldn't let you die," Mrs. Lupis said. "The Society has invested too much in you."

"We're not monsters," her partner said. "We only study them."

"Thank you for not letting me die," I said sarcastically.

"You're quite welcome," they said in unison.

"As for reducing your chance of getting killed by the coven, however, that is your responsibility," Mrs. Lupis added.

"By the way," said Mr. Lopez, "you never found the human-horse hybrid for us."

"Well, you see—"

"No worries." He smiled. "We had lunch at his restaurant yesterday."

"You're okay with him remaining free?"

"After eating food so delicious, how could we not be?"

"We interviewed him and are satisfied that he is responsible enough to hide his extraordinary appearance," Mrs. Lupis said. "He promised to take great care, as do the trolls, ogres, and other monsters who live among humans despite not looking fully human. A centaur, though, is pushing the limits."

"What about Pete, the elephant hybrid?" I asked. "Will he ever be able to live in human society?"

"What do *you* think?"

"I guess not."

My handlers exchanged looks, as if they were communicating telepathically with each other.

"Would you like to visit him?" Mrs. Lupis asked me.

"At the cryptid sanctuary?"

My handlers nodded.

"We think you've earned the right to experience the Society's crown jewel."

"Thank you. I would very much like to see the sanctuary. Where, exactly, is it?"

"It's far away, but just around the corner," Mr. Lopez replied with a wink.

"Okay. . ."

"We can go there now. You drive, and we'll give you directions."

I returned to my car, and my handlers both got into the rear seat, as if I were a cabbie or ride-share driver.

"Go to the Wikowackee Wildlife Preserve," Mr. Lopez said. "We'll direct you from there."

This sounded odd, but I assumed they would take me to a farm or ranch in the rural land surrounding the preserve. Unexpectedly, they told me to turn into the public entrance to the preserve.

I'd hiked the walking paths and kayaked the paddling trails in here and couldn't fathom where the cryptid sanctuary would be. The thousands of acres I hadn't visited were waterways for fishing and miles of marshes and sloughs filled with sawgrass and cattails. There was no land that would have been suitable for building the sanctuary.

As I drove slowly down the only stretch of paved road, which led to the visitors' center, Mr. Lopez told me to take a right on a dirt road. I didn't remember seeing this road before. It was bumpy and wound through cypress trees. Before long, the road ended at a small creek and a wall of sawgrass.

I stopped. "Now what?"

"Keep going."

"How? There's no more road."

"You take your foot off the brake, and put it on the accelerator."

"He's serious," Mrs. Lupis said. "Drive straight ahead through the creek and into the sawgrass."

There was a hint of magic in the air. I drove slowly toward the creek as I'd been told, and the magic increased, making my skin and scalp tingle.

I finally understood that our passage into the sanctuary would not be conventional.

Going against my normal human reluctance, I drove into the creek. It was shallower than expected, and as we rolled up the opposite bank, the wall of sawgrass opened like a gate, revealing a dirt road stretching through the grass.

I drove a hundred yards farther between walls of grass until the walls disappeared and I pulled into the parking lot of what looked like a luxury resort.

"Welcome to the Friends of Cryptids Sanctuary and Research Institute," Mrs. Lupis said with pride. "Park by the front door of the Learning Center, and let's go inside."

The building was modern and new, air-conditioned, and rather attractive. There were dozens of stations with interactive digital media, such as maps, illustrations, and videos. It was like what you'd find in a museum or science center.

"On another occasion, you should spend a day here in the Learning Center," Mrs. Lupis said. "You'll find it very illuminating."

We walked past a life-sized replica of a Skunk Ape, Florida's version of Bigfoot.

"Are there skunk apes living in the sanctuary?" I asked.

"Of course. Several."

In the rear of the facility, double glass doors led to the sanctuary itself. An ogre sat at the wheel of an extended-length golf cart.

Mrs. Lupis introduced me to the driver, Max. The three of us got into the cart, and it rolled along an asphalt path. Again, the place looked like a resort with its lush landscaping, but also like a college campus.

Mr. Lopez pointed to a large neoclassical building.

"That's where the Society keeps its records of all cryptids, going back hundreds of years."

Next, we passed a modern, four-story building with walls of glass.

"That building houses labs for research and observation. The brick building next to it is the hospital for injured or sick cryptids."

As Max drove us deeper into the property, the cryptids themselves came into view. Four trolls played on a golf putting green.

"Many of the cryptids you'll see today are species that also exist in the outside world, like trolls," Mrs. Lupis explained. "The ones who live in the sanctuary found it too stressful having to hide their true natures from humans, or they're recovering from traumatic incidents."

We also saw ogres, pixies, fauns, unicorns, a griffin, and a skunk ape wandering casually through the property, playing horseshoes and lawn bowling, or lounging by the swimming pool. The latter three species I had never seen before, and my heart quickened.

"This is amazing," I said.

We approached a high-rise residential building with balconies.

"I can't believe how big the sanctuary is and that it's right here in Jellyfish Beach."

"Who said it's in Jellyfish Beach?" Mr. Lopez asked. "Remember, it's right around the corner, but also far away. How far, exactly, I cannot say."

"Cannot or will not?"

"Both."

My handlers stepped out of the golf cart and walked briskly toward the entrance to the residential tower. I scrambled to keep up with them, warily walking beneath a tree limb where a Chupacabra lounged. A doorman greeted us at the door. He had the feral eyes of a shifter, but I couldn't tell what kind.

In the gorgeous lobby, Pete rose from a leather sofa to greet us. His trunk rose as he trumpeted with excitement.

"Have you been happy here?" Mrs. Lupis asked him.

"You bet! I don't have to hide from humans anymore, and everyone here is very accepting. The video arcade is awesome!"

"Hi, Pete," I said meekly.

"Oh, hi. Sorry I attacked you in the garage. It was just my fight-or-flight response."

"No worries. I'm glad to hear that you're happy."

"Yeah. I finally feel like I fit in. The food's good, too."

"Yes, it is, indeed," Mr. Lopez said with a wistful smile. "I miss it sometimes."

"You used to work here?" I asked.

"I lived here. Same with Mrs. Lupis. That was before we worked as partners in the real world."

"I don't understand. You lived here while you trained or researched? Were you residential advisors?"

"We were residents, taking sanctuary here," Mrs. Lupis said.

It took a few seconds for me to process this.

"You mean you guys are cryptids?"

"We cannot and will not say."

My mind reeled. Odd as they were, my handlers had always seemed 100 percent human. Now, I had to accept the reality they were not.

But what were they? The tight-lipped expressions they wore told me I would not learn any more from them on this topic, at least not today. That didn't stop the questions from bubbling to the surface of my mind.

Were they shifters? What kind?

Did they appear human because of magic, or was this their natural look?

And did they have families?

There was much I hoped to learn someday, I thought, while Max drove us in the cart back to the Learning Center.

"We brought you here today because we wanted you to see how much importance the Society puts into the welfare of cryptids," Mrs. Lupis said. "We must maintain their secrecy, but we're obligated to understand them and help them thrive."

"The rare bad apples who cause harm must be removed from the population," her partner said. "If we can't drive them away from civilization, we confine them in a facility here. If they're too violent for that. . ."

"They must be put down," I said. "I knew that."

"Which is why it was important that you saw this place—the ideal habitat for cryptids who can't or won't coexist with human society."

"Thank you," I said. "Can the sanctuary take in our devil crab?"

"Your were-crab hasn't molted back into human form yet?"

"No. And she's crabbier than ever."

"I think she'll do just fine continuing to live in the outside world."

When we returned to my car, the drive out was the reverse experience of our drive in. The dense sawgrass closed in and covered the road behind us until it became a wall again after I drove back across the creek.

Once we had returned to familiar settings, it was hard to believe the sanctuary actually existed. But I would never forget it.

After we got to my house, Mrs. Lupis and Mr. Lopez walked away down the street.

"Be prepared for your next assignment," she called back to me.

I swear they disappeared before my eyes when they reached the end of the block.

In the botanica's parking lot, a large shadow covered my car, but I didn't see anything blocking the sun.

The shadow was shaped like an elephant.

"Percy? Are you using your invisibility power?"

Yes. The zombie is inside the shop, his voice rang in my head. *I didn't want to scare him again.*

"Thank you for your thoughtfulness."

Remember, I have a human brain. Well, at least a human cerebral cortex. The rest of my brain must manage all the elephant parts of my body.

"You're very well-educated."

Well-educated for an elephant. Is that what you're thinking?

"Yes. I mean, elephants can't go to school."

Jules and Igor tutored me. They wanted me to go into their scamming operation using my voice only, but they overlooked one serious problem.

"What?"

Elephants can't tell lies.

"I didn't realize that."

Yes. It's one of the many ways we're superior to humans.

"Good to know."

We also never forget, he said, a glimpse of his eyes appearing through his invisibility glamouring. *I can't get you out of my mind.*

"That's very sweet, but—"

Don't say we can only be friends.

"You're an elephant. A very smart, kind, um, good-looking elephant. We can't be more than friends."

Our hearts and souls are what matter. Not our bodies.

"You're such a romantic elephant, but—"

No buts. Someday, you will reciprocate my love, but we'll talk no more about it now.

"I promise I'll visit you regularly at the safari park, but you shouldn't escape from there so often. It's unsafe for you, and the personnel there are very upset, I'm sure."

You didn't mind my escaping when I saved you from Igor.

"That's true. I'll always be grateful for that."

It wasn't easy for me to gore him. He was like family to me.

"I understand. You're a hero to me."

I will return to the park now. Until we meet again.

The shadow across the parking lot disappeared.

Then, the back door of the botanica opened.

"Who are you talking to out here?" Luisa asked.

"The elephant hybrid. He can't stay away from me."

"That is so weird."

A moan came from inside the store. It was Carl.

"We have a zombie hanging out in our workplace. We regularly encounter monsters who are supposed to be nothing other than folklore. And you call what I was doing weird?"

"Good point. Anyway, there's a customer inside asking for powdered unicorn horn. Can you assist her, please?"

If I've learned one thing, it's that in Jellyfish Beach, "weird" is not a pejorative. It's a way of life.

WHAT'S NEXT

The Biggest Bad Wolf

When a city commissioner dies in a suspicious house fire, the Friends of Cryptids Society orders me to investigate his death. Why? Because it turns out he was a werewolf—but not just any werewolf. He was a loup-garou, a monster shifter that makes werewolves look like cuddly lapdogs.

The list of suspects is long, because the commissioner was harassing local businesspeople to exact political retribution. And while Matt and I uncover evidence of a twisted conspiracy, we put our lives in danger. As if my survival wasn't already at risk, thanks to my mother, the black-magic sorceress, who is trying to force me to join her coven.

Why can't I just stick to my simple life of running a

botanica while using my witchcraft to care for aging supernaturals? Why can't Matt and I dip our toes in the pool of romance, instead of watching our backs for monsters?

Welcome to Jellyfish Beach, a wacky world of murder, magic, and mayhem.

Look for *Werewolf Art Thou?* on Amazon or at wardparker.com

Sign up for my newsletter

Get a free novella when you join my occasional newsletter filled with updates on new releases, special deals, and amusing content. All you have to do is visit my website, wardparker.com

ACKNOWLEDGMENTS

I wish to thank my loyal readers, who give me a reason to write more every day. I'm especially grateful to Sharee Steinberg and Shelley Holloway for all your editing and proofreading brilliance. To my A Team (you know who you are), thanks for reading and reviewing my ARCs, as well as providing good suggestions. And to my wife, Martha, thank you for your moral support, Beta reading, and awesome graphic design!

ABOUT THE AUTHOR

Ward is also the author of the Memory Guild midlife paranormal mystery thrillers, as well as the Freaky Florida series, set in the same world as Monsters of Jellyfish Beach, with Missy, Matt, Agnes, and many other familiar characters.

Ward lives in Florida with his wife, several cats, and a demon who wishes to remain anonymous.

Connect with him on social media: Twitter (@wardparker), Facebook (wardparkerauthor), BookBub, Goodreads, or check out his books at wardparker.com

PARANORMAL BOOKS BY WARD PARKER

Freaky Florida Humorous Paranormal Novels

Snowbirds of Prey

Invasive Species

Fate Is a Witch

Gnome Coming

Going Batty

Dirty Old Manatee

Gazillions of Reptilians

Hangry as Hell (novella)

Books 1-3 Box Set

The Memory Guild Midlife Paranormal Mystery Thrillers

A Magic Touch (also available in audio)
The Psychic Touch (also available in audio)
A Wicked Touch (also available in audio)
A Haunting Touch
The Wizard's Touch
A Witchy Touch
A Faerie's Touch
The Goddess's Touch
The Vampire's Touch
An Angel's Touch
A Ghostly Touch (novella)
Books 1-3 Box Set (also available in audio)

Monsters of Jellyfish Beach Paranormal Mystery Adventures

The Golden Ghouls
Fiends With Benefits
Get Ogre Yourself
My Funny Frankenstein
Werewolf Art Thou?

Made in United States
North Haven, CT
14 September 2024

57410709R00168